CU00433589

About the Author

Jason Cobley was born in Devon of Welsh parents and now lives in Warwickshire with his wife, daughter, dog and two intrepid rabbits. Jason studied English Language and Literature at university and has been a teacher for thirty years.

Jason is otherwise known for his novel *A Hundred Years for Arras* based on his relative Robert Gooding Henson, which is linked to some of the short stories in this anthology.

The Mines of Arras and other stories

J.M.Cobley

RECLINING DOG PRESS

This edition first published in 2022
Reclining Dog Press
All rights reserved

© J.M. Cobley, 2022

The right of J.M. Cobley to be identified as the author of this work has been
asserted in accordance with Section 77 of the Copyright, Designs and
Patents Act 1988. No part of this publication may be copied, reproduced,
stored in a retrieval system, or transmitted, in any form or by any means
without the prior permission of the publisher, nor be otherwise circulated in
any form or binding or cover other than that in which it is published and
without a similar condition being imposed on the subsequent purchaser.

This book is a work of fiction and, except in the case of historical fact, any
resemblance to actual persons, living or dead, is purely coincidental.

For those who have lost.

INTRODUCTION

Three of the short stories in this collection are in fact revised sections from my novel *A Hundred Years to Arras*. They feature secondary characters from the book that were cut because it was felt that they didn't contribute much to the overall narrative. It turned out to be a great editing decision as it improved the book immeasurably. But those characters still have stories to be told.

A Hundred Years to Arras was based on a relative who fought at the Battle of Arras in France in 1917. In this collection, *A Goose for Christmas* focuses on one of his ancestors, who was indeed arrested and had to go to court as in the story. Flora's War expands on a nurse from the Voluntary Aid Detachment who features in the novel, as does William, the hero of *The Mines of Arras*. Both provide us with side stories that exist alongside the narrative of *A Hundred Years to Arras*. You don't have to have read it to enjoy these stories, though.

Most of the remaining short stories originally appeared in a collection I put out a few years ago called *Moving Targets*, which is now out of print, although *Missiles* and *Bits* were created separately.

A GOOSE FOR CHRISTMAS

In 1668, the court was in session. With no official court buildings in this corner of the parish, the visiting magistrate had taken temporary command of the back room of The Boot Inn. The ancient parish of Taunton St James covered a wide area, but neither the plaintiff nor defendant were willing to travel. Magistrate Bellweather was a wizened yew tree branch of a man who was hot in his black tunic and the fashionable but inconvenient frills. He placed his heap of papers on the scrubbed table and took a seat. He declined the proffered cup of ale with a glare, despite it being a warm June day.

'Most people being here now come to town, I call this court to session. Be advised, gentlemen, I am not best amused by having to call court to order in this inn. I therefore expect this to be concluded in short time and we can all go on to wherever we intend to sup tonight. I have not eaten all day, so my patience must not be tried,' he said. 'I will see the first witness now.'

His cap wrung like a rag in his hands, Augustine Sellwood took the stand, which is to say he stood up. He did this with some effort, for he was a sweaty, rotund man with a leg that trailed behind him whenever he walked from inn to stile and back again. Introductions done, Bellweather said, 'I am given to understand that you are the plaintiff, Mister Sellwood?'

'Aye.'

'Do speak. Don't let me hold you back.'

'Well, the light were a bit dimpsey at the end of the day. It were a gurt job, taking down my standing.'

'This was at Taunton fayre?'

'Aye.'

'Go on.'

'It were in the way of where Henson wanted to go, so he started spuddling. I just wanted to pack up and go home.'

'This is Roger Henson?'

'Aye.'

'So, what did he do, man? Get to it!'

'He kicked over the posts and ripped all my cloths and that.'

'With one kick?'

'Aye.'

'And you are seeking compensation?'

'Sir?'

'You want money,' Bellweather sighed.

'Aye.'

Sellwood was relieved to be able to sit down. Roger Henson, a broad man with gnarled hands from heavy work, strode in late. He quickly recovered his breath, apologised to the magistrate, and stood to attention. Bellweather was easily impressed by less easy manners, so resolved to end things quickly. 'You are a carpenter, Mister Henson?' he asked.

'Yes, sir. I have taken employment in carpentry this past ten year or so in and around Taunton St James.'

'I gather your workmanship has been praised by many.'

'I hope so, sir.'

'Yet, you attacked Mister Sellwood's standing, splintering his wooden posts.'

'Aye, sir. He had employed me to build it for him but did not pay. He were selling brawn and pies and I think all his money went into that, so he never paid me. I went to see him at the end of the day to see if he would pay me what he owed from his earnings. He said he had none. It were a gurt liberty. I'd done a proper job and all. I admit he made me angry, he did.'

'So, you decided to teach him a lesson?'

'Not exactly. I just got angry, sir. It weren't right. There's right and wrong, and this was wrong, in my eyes.' Roger Henson was unapologetic.

Bellweather took no more time to deliberate than it did for him to finally accept a cup of ale and drain it to the dregs. With a belch, he said, 'Sellwood, you will pay the man or spend a day in the stocks and then still have to pay him. Henson, you will moderate your temper and rebuild the standing for no additional coin after Mister Sellwood has paid you.'

Roger Henson left the back room of the inn that day with a measure of dignity but a sense of injustice that he passed on through his family.

In 1784, Roger's grandson James Henson was born. James married Mary Gooding, and together they had nine children. The eldest, John, was born in 1809 and, on the penultimate day in December 1861, the rhythm of history took an extra beat as he stood before the Justices of the Peace at Combe Flory, charged with stealing one goose. The bird in question was the property of George Webber, a local farmer. As if that were not enough to face, on the same day he was simultaneously charged with stealing one live sheep from William Dibble of West Bagborough, another farmer.

John Henson wept with anger, his fingers wrapped up in his hair, as he stood in the dock. Justice of the Peace Carew addressed him directly.

'State your name and profession,' he said.

'John Henson, farm labourer.'

'How do you plead, Henson?'

John pounded the door of the cottage with his fists. He wrenched at the latch to no avail; his fingers could get no purchase in the dark, and his pockets were empty of keys. He hammered with the side of his fist. It was a dull mallet that thudded against the door but achieved nothing except pushing his wife's patience to the edge.

'Jane,' he said. 'Let me in. It's John.'

'I know who it is,' came the reply from the other side of the door. 'Stop your banging. You'll wake the baby.'

'Let me in.'

'No. You're drunk again.'

'No, I'm not. I mean, aye, I probably am, but I got something.'

There was the rattle of a key from inside, and the easy creaking of the door as it swung inwards. Mary Jane Henson, in her nightgown and threadbare cap, held a candle in her hand. Six-year-old Harriet, already learning to look at her father with disdain, stood with her mother. Two-year-old Albyn was inside with baby Tom, a protective arm around his brother of four months.

'What is it?' Jane said, wearily.

With a flourish, John revealed the sheep, a docile young ewe, standing beside him. A rope was loosely tied around her neck, with the other end looped around his wrist. Under his arm was tucked a much less conscious goose, its neck drooping heavily like a wet sock.

'Dinner,' he replied, proudly.

Young Harriet echoed her mother's words when she put her head in her hands and sighed, 'Not again.'

On the thirtieth day of December, John, with his best shirt an inch too short on the sleeve and without a collar, bowed his head humbly when the Justice of the Peace asked him to state his name and occupation. Justice Carew asked him for his plea. Only a fool would have denied the goose feathers swept into corners on the scullery floor; only a fool would have denied the sheep that grazed, tied to a post outside the cottage all night into the morning.

'Not guilty,' John pled. He spent New Year in Taunton gaol.

FLORA'S WAR

It was December 1916, and Flora was one of a dozen Voluntary Aid Detachment nurses at the field hospital in Northern France. Just twenty-two years old, she had already resisted all her landowner father's attempts to find her a husband. Whilst entirely respectable men all, the one thing that marked them out was that they had not gone to war. Each had a perfectly good reason for not doing so, especially those excused for medical reasons, but none of them struck her as husband material. When all was said and done, nobody really ever struck her as husband material.

A year earlier, the Quantock Hills spread out before Flora like an exquisite, quilted blanket. The rocky Jurassic coastline spread, climbing over itself, where the farmland undulated between steep, deep, wooded narrow valleys. At the summits of heathland, heather and gorse grew amongst bracken dotted with whortleberry and the sounds of birds. Flora would often go out riding alone, dismount and sit with an apple, listening and watching for the skylarks, linnets and warblers that sang a serenade just for her.

In summers, she would sometimes see a nightjar when the light was right, and butterflies would flit in and out of the heather. In winters, as now, she would often see a hen harrier gliding over, low in search of prey. This morning, with the frost crunchy underfoot, Flora had left home as soon as dawn was creaking open the day. The early winter was fresh and clear.

She sat comfortably, her thighs well used to gripping the sides of her saddle on the broad back of her horse, Barabbas. The name had been her choice. Naming her horse after a Biblical insurrectionist who went to his death alongside Jesus, punished for his rebellion against Pontius Pilate, suited her vision of herself. Barabbas was of course eventually freed by Pilate, who kept Jesus locked up instead. He had gotten away with it. She liked the idea that she and Barabbas would, from time to time, get away with things that young ladies were not meant to do. She was well aware of her privilege, and when she rode out into the villages, it did not always sit well with her when she rode above the people slopping out their houses, their grubby children so excited to see Barabbas.

Barabbas' strong shoulders and wide chest made him seem as if he was strutting, ready for a fight, especially when he was obliged to stand still, snorting in the winter air. He was a little short in the back, but that made him comfortable to ride in trot.

She waited for the hen harrier to circle up and away, then she kicked him on gently. As a gelding, he was far calmer than he sometimes appeared: she liked how appearances could sometimes be made to be deceptive. He was an iron-grey hunter, with a neatly pulled mane and tail that matched her own ponytail. When she rode along, she preferred to let the curls of her unruly hair do their own thing beneath her hat, rather than bunch up, tightly wound like all the other ladies in her circle. Barabbas picked up pace, his feet like dinner plates slamming onto the hard ground between the bracken and gorse.

Flora steadfastly refused to ride side-saddle. She was wearing jodhpurs, hunter boots and her father's old jacket that morning. With a wry smile to herself, she thought about how her father may make a show of disapproval in front of others but would secretly approve of his daughter's rebelliousness. He was the one, after all, who encouraged her to prepare for university. Mother had been busy planning a route to marriage, bloodline, and grandchildren, which Flora had not exactly ignored but had also not engaged with particularly. She saw her own future as somewhere between the two. Her father's drive to educate his daughter had brought an eclectic clutch of books into her hands, not least of which ranged from Mary

Woolstencraft to George Bernard Shaw. She would be inclined to beat the drum for the suffragists, but she often felt that they were missing a trick. Her own deeds were not going to need extravagant, confrontational words to back them up. She was just going to do them.

It was still early enough in the morning to see grazing red deer on the heath before they retreated to scrub and woodland. A single female deer was grazing on a slope. As Barabbas huffed, still many yards away, she looked up, listening, eyes focused on something far away. The deer leapt into action and pranced down the slope towards the combe and wooded cover. She was soon lost to sight as the morning mist lingered where Flora and Barabbas stood.

How wonderful would it be to jaunt with the deer, to leave behind the expectations of life, to gallop into the mist, to be lost to all but the circling eye of the hen harrier? When Flora cast her own eye over her own life, she saw a beautiful home adorned with an array of beautiful dresses, a nanny and then a governess, and then a finishing education amongst other smart young ladies with dreams of husbands and country piles. But she did not see herself within it. She was an observer only, a reader of the diary of a country lady, soon to be a debutante.

Galloping across the heath, her hair flaring like a flag, she imagined a different future.

Flora's future was one in which she did not even contemplate a husband; why should she pin all her hopes on a man? Of course, she knew the answer: it was expected. But, in these uncertain times of war, with the fields and towns emptying of men, how many would remain for her to choose from? She was determined, no matter what her mother may have intimated, that the choice would be hers.

It was with this in mind, a screwed-down resolve to determine her own path in life, that Flora Stuckey stood in her father's study in her jodhpurs, riding crop still in hand after the morning's ride.

'This won't do, Flora,' said her father.

'To what are you referring, Father?' she replied.

The tone of exaggerated deference was one that she knew infuriated him; nevertheless, it was the tone she had taken. This was a road frequently travelled in the Stuckey household.

'You know very well. Your mother tells me that you are keen to sign up as a... nurse.' There was the hint of a sneer on his face at the last word.

'Yes,' she said simply. And waited.

Walter Stuckey shuffled some papers on his desk nervously. He was used to robust conversations with his employees and contractors, but they were always men. His daughter was a quite different proposition altogether.

'Your mother has not expressed a view, but I can imagine what it is.'

Flora smiled. Her mother and she were not always of one mind, but she knew by now that a proposal would never be placed under her father's gaze for perusal unless the outcome had already been decided.

'Yes,' she said again.

'I am very wary.'

'I know.'

'You have not yet met a husband.'

'Perhaps I could find one in France.'

He shot her a gaze, like a blunt dart aimed by a blind man; it was never going to pierce its target. 'But you... you are not a nurse,' he said, after a pause.

'They'll train me.'

Her father nodded. He ran a hand over his entirely bald head, as if refreshing the argument. He took a seat at his desk and motioned for Flora to take a seat in the adjacent armchair.

She complied, crossed her legs casually, and smiled disarmingly.

Thus disarmed, he sank back into his chair. 'Flora,' he began.

'Yes, Father?'

'This is not a respectable occupation for a lady. It is arduous and a strain on the nerves.'

She laughed abruptly, covered her mouth with her hand. Taking a breath with more composure, she replied, 'Do I really look that delicate to you, Father? Have I ever been? Honestly?'

'No, of course not. The child of Walter Stuckey is not meant to be some man's decoration. We will find you a husband that matches your temperament, of course. And an education will be yours. I require that of you. Flora, you do not need to mire yourself in the blood of injured men and the sweat of gin-soaked domestics to prove yourself to me.'

'I'm sure there are some nurses who have never partaken of gin, and they may even bathe regularly.'

Stuckey put his forehead in the palms of his hands; this was more of his headstrong daughter's sarcasm. He had come to dread her barbs, for he rarely had any defence. He suffering in his support of suffrage as he was often a minority voice at the gentlemen's club. However, scrubbing elbow-deep in blood and carbolic was not necessarily the vision he had for his daughter's future.

In fact, the sort of women who were joining the Voluntary Aid Detachment were from all levels of society. Far from the romantic image of Florence Nightingale and her mythical lamp, however, the urgency and speed with which nursing services had to be established for the battlefields left so many nurses poorly trained. It would be several years until uniform standards of training would be established. For now, the hotch-potch merging of military and civilian nursing services meant that the call went out far and wide for women to sign up to be trained in caring for the sick and wounded troops in France.

'This will not be for the faint-hearted, Flora,' he said, finally.

'Good then.' Yes, indeed. There was little that could be described as faint-hearted about his daughter.

'Sometimes, I do wonder whether our baby was exchanged for that of some Viking warrior. Your friends are more concerned with their deportment than their deployment.'

'Drinking tea rather than swimming in blood?'

'Quite. Your mother approves?'

'Yes.'

'And there is no changing your mind?'

'No.'

'Why?'

'Because this world is mine as well as yours. It belongs to women as much as it does men. It belongs to the poor as well as the rich. If I sit by with my sewing and afternoon tea, I don't deserve to be part of what follows. That is, if any good at all can come of the whole enterprise.'

Stuckey moved from behind his desk, his thumbs thrust into his waistcoat pockets. He simply nodded. He had lost but his lack of resistance spoke more of pride in his daughter than any words ever could.

Flora joined the Order of St John Ambulance and was soon deployed into France, where the training focused as much on the perception that the nurses would be wayward and wanton if left to their own devices as how to dress a wound. 'Modesty of mind and modesty of speech' were emphasised by Matron, Flora and the others were shown how to sweep up, mop up all kinds of rancid liquids, treat suppurating wounds and administer the few medicines that they had access to. No amount of preparation, however, prepared her fully for the stench that came with gas gangrene and trench foot. It was sometimes a lottery whether she would be mopping up vomit from the soldiers or the nurses. Either one was equally likely.

Training was perfunctory to begin with. Flora was lined up with two other young women opposite a line of established nurses, some of whom were professionals, in that this had always been their employment and they were somewhat resentful of having been shifted abroad and rolled in with volunteer amateurs. A much greater division was with the military nurses, who were invariably male medics who functioned as part of their regiments. It was a confusing introduction for Flora.

Matron was a woman of broad buttocks and narrow opinions, who brandished her forearms like rolling pins and barked in a clipped fashion that she had acquired from the military doctors – all men, of course - that gave her orders.

'What is your name?' she said by way of introduction.

Flora removed her hat and pin, allowing herself to loosen her hair. 'Flora Stuckey,' she replied.

'We'll be putting that hat to one side and tying that hair up with the correct attire.' Matron gave her no more acknowledgement before turning to the woman who stood beside her, little more than a girl. 'And you?'

'Beth Dibble,' blushed the girl, shorter than Flora, rounder and ruddy-cheeked. She reddened even further with embarrassment, the blush reaching to her ears and clump of unruly curls. Matron stared. 'Elizabeth Dibble,' Beth clarified. Matron nodded gravely, then turned her piercing gaze to the third girl.

As thin as a riding crop, pinched and biting her lip, she introduced herself without being asked. 'I am Clara Wisden, Matron. Pleased to meet you,' she said, putting out her hand.

Matron gently moved Clara's hand to one side with the back of hers. 'That's because you don't know me yet, young lady.'

The field hospital was constructed from prefabricated huts, shipped to France from England, comprising wards for officers, wards for men, and the smallest private spaces for the nurses that Flora could have imagined. Her cubicle was fine for sleeping, but the bare walls and rudimentary bunk made her long for the open air, galloping across the heath with Barabbas and nothing but her own romantic dreams of service. The reality was more mundane. Flora, Clara, Beth, and a slightly older nurse who took the girls under her wing, named Maud Marley, soon fell into a routine that left them elbow deep in dying flesh and bodily fluids day after day.

So many men came under Flora's care and died after sepsis set in. It seemed unavoidable, a curse that stalked them throughout the war. The bacillus that caused gas gangrene, spawned by the disease in trenches that were often little more than latrines, was worse. It certainly smelled like hell. Matron warned the nurses against having too much sympathy for the men, however. They were banned from wearing anything other than their uniforms and to be wary of sympathetic attentions from the men. Like Flora's mother, Matron seemed to just assume that she was on the lookout for a husband. Some of the other nurses may well have been, but not Flora.

A tearful goodbye to her parents had already been shoved to the back of her mind, buried under a heap of instructions and orders, building a framework of behaviour to live by. Self-restraint was the order of each and every day. After all, according to Matron, they were doing this to glorify God. That was not quite the way that Flora saw things. There was nothing that she saw when holding the hands of screaming amputees or mopping up the blood and vomit from poison gas victims that glorified God, or even hinted that God was watching.

Nevertheless, daily polishing of her shoes, buckles and badges were to glorify God. Daily abstention from wearing make-up, jewellery, or anything other than uniform, was to glorify God. Saying Grace before every meal was to glorify God. Saying morning prayers on the ward was to glorify God. Saying evening prayers on the ward was to glorify God. Looking after the men's wellbeing was to glorify God. The last one was the hardest for Flora. For Flora, it seemed increasingly that God had abandoned these men. Still, she had to admire Matron's unstinting faith. Sometimes it seemed that Matron would even see doing one's business at the latrines as glorifying God.

Matron was not always such a fury. One evening, Flora was alone in her cubicle, staring quietly at the shadows. Matron passed by the open door, paused, then looked in.

'Nurse Stuckey?'

'Matron.'

'What are you doing?'

'I'm off duty, Matron. I was preparing for bed. I know I could be on call in the night. I wanted to get some sleep...'

Matron waved the words away and stepped into the room. 'That is not what I meant, Flora. I meant, what are you doing?' she repeated, slowly.

'Nothing.'

'Praying?'

Flora could not quite suppress her nervous laughter, tried to cover it as a cough, realising it was inappropriate and not reflecting what she actually felt. 'A man died a few minutes ago. I was...'

'Oh, yes. The officer. The one with the infection?'

'No. Private Ellis. His... his was the stomach wound.'

Matron winced, sat down beside Flora on her cot. 'There was little we could do.'

'He tried to hold his... intestines in with his hand,' Flora said, closing her eyes against the image.

'You were beside him. That was important, Flora.'

'He wanted me to pray with him.'

'And did you?'

The tears came quietly, long rivulets scarring her cheeks. 'No,' Flora replied.

Matron did not speak for a moment. Flora could sense some confusion from her. Or was it anger? Irritation? Whichever it was, her words, when they came, were simple. 'Then, next time, you must.'

'Must I? Is God even listening?'

Matron got to her feet, went to the door. 'You are not doing it for God. Or even yourself. Do it for the men.'

When it came time for lights out, and time for sleep, Flora undressed slowly. Each layer of her uniform was laid out flat on her coat before being folded over the back of a chair. She smoothed the day's wrinkles out of her pinafore, picking pieces of fluff. A stray spot of something greasy marred the front. She scrubbed at it vainly; it would have to wait for the week's wash.

The hem was weighed down with the mud and stains of the day. Much of it would dry and flake off by morning, but some would remain, a red-brown remnant of a man's suffering. She dressed for bed, let her hair down and devoted a vital few minutes to brush it through. This was a few minutes for her alone. She would much rather have brushed it through wet, but traipsing down the narrow corridor to fill a jug with water and tip it into a basin in her cupboard-like room just to tend to her curls was not really worth the effort when all she would be able to manage was a few hours of sleep before she would be raised by Matron again in the morning.

Flora used to pride herself on being someone who was not flattered by flattery. Her head of hair was for function, not adornment, especially as it often spent most of the day clamped under a riding hat. But, here in France, where private moments of self-care were so rare, she seized on anything that helped remind her that she was something other than a human slop-bucket and bath sponge. Her hair, almost matted in places, managed the impressive feat of being both dry and greasy at the same time. She longed for a long, hot bath. Inserting herself under the covers, she laid back and tried to imagine being in a steamy, soapy bath. Her muscles would not quite relax enough, her limbs tense, her stomach tight, ever on alert for an alarm call to tend to another sudden inrush of patients. Matron called them patients, but Flora could only see broken men and damaged boys. Some were eviscerated in their minds and intact in their bodies; some were the reverse.

If God was indeed interested as Matron suggested, his was a detached observance. A God at arm's length did not deserve her prayers, she decided in that cold night under a blanket so thin that she guessed one wash would render it transparent.

Lying in her cot whilst other nurses chattered, Flora stared into the darkness as if looking for the silently observing God in the shadows. When she fell asleep, she had not yet found Him, and neither did she think she would.

The commanding officer of their hospital was a Colonel Warwick. He was a medical man, highly attentive to detail but entirely inflexible in his view of the roles of the women and surgical procedures. This was a man who had distinguished himself in the Boer War but now, even in 1917, with his upright back, tidy moustache and fastidious cleaning and operating routines, he had yet to adjust to the true horror of injuries that the trenches threw up for them on a daily basis. Flora admired and was frustrated by him in equal measure.

The bridge between the women and Colonel Warwick was the dashing Captain Brooks, a public-school rugby man who had only just taken his medical degree when war broke out. Beth became very observant and eager to please whenever he came near, which entertained the others no end. If he were not oblivious to the female attention, he made no show of it, which made Beth flutter her eyelashes in his direction even more.

Months passed at the hospital, the year turned to 1917, and the February rains afforded scant opportunity for enjoying the open air. The relentless cycle of tending to the injured and the insane, as Matron described it, had become all that Flora knew. Each day alternated between feeding, cleaning, bandaging and comforting men who were little more than pale bags of muscle who had less control over their bowels than their hands. Her hands were deep in the abrasive water of harsh soap and dissolving dirt as she scrubbed at nurse's uniforms soiled with the blood and vomit of men reduced to dribbling babies in their cots.

The skin around Flora's knuckles was red, rubbed, and raw. The water, although only lukewarm, stung her where cracks in her skin exposed the flesh. She had not counted on this. She had imagined herself a no-nonsense antidote to the simpering girls that rallied round the mannered officers and handsome privates. She had run from home, where 'husband' was the word that rang in her ears from dawn to dusk, to here, where sometimes the only words to be heard were screams of pain and anguish.

Flora dropped a pinafore, heavy with the weight of water, back into the bucket with the scrubbing brush. She held her hands before her like claws. Even elbow deep in horse manure and sodden straw, she had never been so stripped of everything that she felt made her who she was. Her lobster claws of hands, the skin puckering and tight, smelled of carbolic. There was nowhere to erase the smell, to clean them and restore any kind of moisture. She let the air bite into the skin, throbbing with the work of washing, washing, washing.

Flora's head bowed as she sank to her knees, her hands held away from her body as if in supplication. Her chest heaved, her breath catching the back of her throat. Deep inside, she was pulling on a thread that had long lain tied up in a tight, complicated knot. She wept. She wept huge, seemingly solid, clumps of despair. Clods of buried needs and disappointments and self-deceit were suddenly dug up. She sobbed and sobbed until she could barely breathe. Great gulps of air and clenching her sore fists helped her pull herself back under control.

The washing splashed and bubbled gently as she idly stirred it, her fingertips dangling in the bucket. Sitting on the floor, her feet tucked under the hefty cloth of her uniform, she gradually recovered her breathing and let herself be quiet for a few moments. Her eyes were open. She was looking at nothing but her other hand, the palm upturned.

'What was I thinking? I shouldn't be here,' she said, knowing nobody was nearby to listen.

Beth appeared in the doorway. 'Flora?'

'I can't do anything to help these men. I can't even do the laundry properly. I don't think I'm capable of anything at all.'

Beth rolled up her sleeves and plunged her hands into the water to resume Flora's work. 'Well, that's probably true. I'm just a Somerset girl, but I can wash some clothes and empty bedpans well enough.'

Flora was getting to her feet, pulling on the back of a chair for support. Standing was never usually this much effort. 'I'm a Somerset girl too,' she said.

'Hmm.'

'What does that mean?'

Beth said nothing and sank a scrubbing brush into the water. She began working on a stubborn stain. 'Well, Flora, your Somerset is all hills and ponies and Daddy's money. Mine isn't.'

Flora blushed. Class was rarely something she considered, and she had no consideration that she might have conveyed any sense of being separate from the other women since she arrived in France. Perhaps, she was realising, she was considering the wrong thing. 'Beth,' she began.

Beth scrubbed away. 'You can make it up to me, fellow Somerset girl and all. Would you do me a service, as a respectable lady?'

Wondering whether Beth was beginning to mock her, Flora paused. 'What is it?' she said.

Abandoning the washing, Beth turned, a slight rosy blush pricking her cheeks, a sudden heat bursting from inside. 'Captain Brooks stopped me in the corridor yesterday. Bold as anything, he was, in front of Matron and all. His eyes were all shiny and he was like a little boy for a moment, all nervous. He gave me some flowers – it was just a posy really, grabbed from along the path outside I expect – but he'd found a little ribbon to wrap the stems up in. I'd have trimmed them myself, but what did he know? Even these officers – especially these officers – wouldn't know these things, I suppose. Anyway, he asked me then and there – right then and there in front of

Matron and all – whether I would care to take tea with him in the town.' Beth finally took a breath and waited for Flora's reaction, seemingly expecting some sort of approbation or applause.

'Well, I'm sure that is perfectly lovely,' said Flora. She could see that Beth was waiting for more questions. She had to fill the role of gossip now: one to which she was not entirely accustomed. 'So… um… what did you say?'

'Well,' Beth replied, 'It was completely unexpected, so I…'

'Was it?'

She blushed again. 'Well… anyway, I said I would be delighted to accompany him into town to take tea.'

'When?'

'Tomorrow.'

'And what is it you want me to do?' Flora was wary now. Tomorrow was her off-duty day too, and she was hopeful to find some time on her own, if she could find a way to explore the countryside without being shot at.

'Be my chaperone, Flora? Please?' Beth did, to be fair, seem reluctant to ask, perhaps aware of how much of an imposition it could be on someone who, after all, she did not know all that well.

Flora sighed, more from tiredness than anything, but a 'yes' followed her exhalation of breath.

'The time may come when you'll need me to return the favour.'

'I doubt it. I came here exactly because I didn't want a husband.'

Beth frowned. 'What kind of woman doesn't want a husband?'

'My kind, perhaps.'

Beth frowned some more. Flora herself was unsure what she meant – it seemed to just feel like the only kind of answer that Beth deserved in that moment - and wanted to avoid having to clarify, so she sent that train of thought into a siding.

Although it was a day off for both of them, Beth was up with the morning reveille.

'A car?' Beth laughed. 'No. He's borrowing the motor ambulance, or rather the driver is taking us in it. He has some supplies to pick up at the same time.' Ordinarily, a trip in the motor ambulance to collect deliveries of medicines, dressings and all the unctions and oils that they needed from time to time, was an exciting adventure. Usually, one of the nurses would be selected to accompany the driver in case they found themselves having to pick up a casualty on the way back. Today, however, it felt like a strange invasion of Beth's mundane obsession into Flora's occasional adventure.

Two o'clock arrived, as did the ambulance. Captain Brooks descended from the passenger seat, his uniform immaculate, his hair freshly and nattily combed, as flat and black as an oil slick. His moustache was newly trimmed, slightly unevenly on one side, which suggested he had completed the job in haste. Involuntarily, Beth gave a little curtsy in greeting. Flora had to press her lips together to suppress a snigger.

The driver, a gruff, frowning, burly private, leaned over to the window. 'Don't hang about.'

Captain Brooks motioned gallantly for the ladies to sit in the back, perched on a bench under the canvas tarpaulin that covered the frame of the back of the ambulance. He returned to the front with the driver, and they set off for an estaminet around the edge of the Grand Place. Much of the town had been shelled, including the town square, but in this transition from winter to spring in early 1917, Arras was under British supervision. After a bumpy but uneventful ride, they disembarked. Brooks and the driver made arrangements for their return whilst the driver headed off to pick up crucial supplies of cigarettes, biscuits, and jam – the staple diet of the hungry Tommy.

A pile of rubble formed a semi-circle around an open wall that had been bolstered with a couple of iron posts. They would not be there for long, as they would be needed elsewhere, but for now they kept the estaminet open to customers. It was of course also open to elements. Two older French women, too old and too stubborn to have evacuated the town when the shelling had started, were serving English tea in pots, along with homemade spongey French 'financier' cakes in the shape of stumpy fingers. Flora marvelled at the ladies' ability to summon up the eggs needed to make the cakes before the Tommies had insisted them all be fried with chips.

Climbing over the remains of the wall, Flora and Beth followed Brooks into the estaminet, the café really only the half-demolished parlour of a once-comfortable French family home. Brooks had clearly been before, as he was greeted warmly by the ladies, and shown to a corner table. Flora sat at an adjacent table whilst Beth and Brooks sat beside each other.

Flora took out a handkerchief and wiped the dust off the surface of her table. She sipped her tea, without milk, from a china teacup that was almost translucent in its delicacy. It was another marvel: how could this fragile thing have survived?

Beth asked inane questions about how 'our side' was faring in battle. Brooks declined to be specific except that things were 'disappointing' and that he was 'hopeful.'

'Have you always been a doctor, Captain?' asked Beth, pouring the tea.

'Yes, for a little time before the war.'

Flora tuned out of the inanity of the conversation, allowing herself to be a radio slipping in and out of signal. She filled the gaps with aimless reverie, imagining herself rising up on the Quantock hills with Barabbas. She picked up snatches of chatter about brothers and sisters, roses in their gardens, hopes for the future and cottages in the country. It was only when Brooks starting pontificating about medicine that she paid closer attention, by which time her tea had gone cold.

Beth had mentioned, with some compassion, a couple of soldiers who she had tended for with ailments that were not physical: soldiers who cried for their mothers at night and shook their heads during the day, sometimes hugging themselves to sleep. One of them flinched at any loud sound. The clatter of bed pans sent him diving under his bed with the spiders and the dust.

Brooks scoffed. 'Bloody malingerers,' he said. Beth blushed a different shade, unsure how to respond. Flora put down her teacup and angled her chair so that she could more easily face the Captain.

'They do seem very upset,' Beth began.

Brooks continued, it seemingly more important that he have his opinion heard than to listen to the nurse. 'It seems to be that these neuralgia sufferers just need the proverbial kick up the backside, so to speak. If it is all in the mind or the nerves as we suspect, we just need a therapy to shock them out of it. There are so many barriers that our men put up themselves to stop them getting better. Some even refuse surgery. Take the Gurkhas. Those darkies refusing amputations.'

'For neuralgia?' Beth was either confused or incredulous. Flora couldn't tell, but she could sense her friend withdrawing from the gallant gentleman who, over tea, was beginning to veer between bore or boor.

'For injuries, of course. Some ballyhoo about wanting to be intact to go to heaven or some such. Not an English heaven, certainly.' He poured himself more tea.

Beth's and Flora's eyes met; the former imploring, the latter set and stony. Flora interrupted, 'Excuse me, Captain Brooks. What sort of therapies are you referring to?'

'First of all, one must regard those wounded in mind as having retreated from the war,' said Brooks, settling into his seat. He had an audience now. 'There is a case for treating these nervous behaviours, the mutism and hysteria, amongst other things, with a shock of some description. Firing squad seems rather final and seems to suggest that these patients are simple cowards rather than malingerers. I have been looking into aversion therapies.'

'To avert them from being poorly?'

He shot Flora a defiant glance. 'There has been some success with applying an electrical current to the affected part: the throat of mutes, for example.'

Beth was silent, sipping her now-cooled tea.

'I thought you were opposed to drastic experimental procedures, Captain,' said Flora.

'Well,' he smiled wryly, idly stirring his tea. 'I think that rather depends on whether it's my procedure or not. When one is in control of others, that's when one can effect the greatest innovation. Something has to stop these men weeping like children and jumping at their own shadows so that we can get them back in the field.'

'At the front?'

'Indeed, yes.'

Beth stood abruptly, nodding to her friend. She buttoned her coat. 'I should like to take our journey back now in the motor ambulance, Captain, sir, if you wouldn't mind.'

Flora echoed her movements. They were ready to go. Still seated, Brooks was nonplussed but quickly gathered up his composure. Nodding assent, he left a few francs for the ladies of the estaminet and led the way back to their lift. Beth and Flora followed behind him, walking together.

Looking at Flora, Beth whispered, 'I don't really understand, but he wasn't really interested in me at all, was he?'

'Beastly,' Flora replied, although she was not yet sure what had disturbed her the most about Captain Brooks that afternoon. In the back of the motor ambulance, during an otherwise mostly silent return journey. Beth abruptly squeezed Flora's hand. 'I don't think this will be the best place to find a husband after all,' she said, then let go.

Flora sighed and drew a great smile of relief.

On other occasions after that, Captain Brooks mentioned how he saw such soldiers as malingerers and spoke at length of aversion therapies that he had heard of and wanted to try. Matron was unwilling, and neither Beth nor Flora had liked the sound of passing electrical currents through men's bodies.

Men passed through their care, some surviving, some not. Some sweet young men, barely more than boys, even wrote to the nurses after they were discharged. When the letters stopped, the women could usually tell what had happened. All the men, she thought, deserved to have someone take their hand through their last steps.

One day in April, on Easter Monday, hidden troops disgorged from Arras to the German front line. By the end of the day, men and boys, the living and the dead, poured into the hospital. Amongst them was a wounded young man, shivering already from blood poisoning, with the voice of old Somerset, who faded in and out of delirium. Flora stayed with him, by his side, attempting prayer, until Beth saw him.

When Beth dropped the empty bedpan, it clattered to the floor, loud enough to wake the other men, but she ignored it. She fell to her knees and took the young man's hand from Flora. 'Bob,' she said, little more than a whisper.

Beth knew him as Bob. Bob from her village. A fleeting sweetheart, a ghost of her past, here now in the hospital. He preferred now to be called Robert, a more assured man than the boy she once knew. Private Robert Gooding Henson's breathing was ragged and his grip weak, but Beth let him hold her hand. Really it was her holding his.

That evening, an angry Private Taylor from the East Lancashires had raged in his bed, his face red with fury at the enemy. Robert had fallen asleep as soon as he had been returned to his bed, but he was now restless. It was not Private Taylor's rantings that disturbed him, however. Rather, it seemed to Beth as if something within was wrestling with his soul.

'What is it now?' Beth had said to Taylor. Across from Taylor, Robert drifted in and out of consciousness, never quite awake and never fully asleep. Next to Taylor, Private Jeffries from the same regiment as Robert, laughed.

'What are you laughing at?' Taylor spat at Jeffries, who looked as if his face would split open along the shrapnel scar along his cheek each time he chuckled.

'You,' he replied, with no shame.

'Now, men,' said Flora, standing between the beds. 'Why are you so angry?'

Without saying a word, Taylor whipped back his stiff blanket to reveal his leg. It was foul-smelling, soporific. Gangrene was eating away at him, his redness as much from fever as from anger.

'Well, that doesn't help, does it? Let me look at it. I'm here to clean your wounds anyway.' Flora was actually on bed bath duty but liked to put it off as long as possible, whenever she could.

'I seen a leg like this before,' he said. 'Out there. I seen it cut off rather than let it get this bad. Cut it off, nurse! Finish what that bastard Bosche started!'

'Now, I can't do that, can I? The surgeon decided we can save it. But...' She paused, seeing the infection. 'I'll see the doctor.'

'Bastard Huns,' Taylor muttered.

Jeffries sat up in his bed, leaning on his elbow. 'Nurse?' he said.

'Yes?' she replied, as she began sponging away at Taylor's leg, avoiding the wound for now.

'Him over there,' he said, nodding at Robert.

'Yes?'

'Think I know him. But it's a big regiment and we all get mixed up with others when we're out there. Somerset lad like me. Think I saw him fighting once. Brave, helping his pals, dragging one of them away from the barbed wire when we couldn't get through. Funny the things you remember, lying here. Most of the time I just remember seeing my pals lying in the dirt for days, maggots crawling in and over them, crows circling overhead, and that stare. The stare of the dead man.' He had stopped laughing and laid back, his eyes closed against the world.

After a moment, Jeffries posed a question. 'Have you ever seen a ghost?' he said.

Flora was applying a fresh bandage to Taylor's leg, so was only half listening. 'What was that?'

'A ghost. Ever seen one?'

'I do not believe so,' she said warily. 'I know some soldiers have claimed they have seen things out on the battlefield. In the sort of miasma that fills the air, I'm not surprised that there are hallucinations from time to time.'

'No, I mean really.'

'We had a young man here a few weeks ago who relayed a story about someone he knew seeing the Angel of Mons, and another had seen an ancient bowman from Agincourt, all before big battles.'

Clara bustled past, hearing the conversation. 'It's all nonsense,' she joined.

'Wait up there, Nurse, and listen. Let me tell you my story,' insisted Jeffries. He had a little twinkle in his eye that made the nurses want to indulge him. The evening was otherwise drawing up its knees to sleep, so Flora said, 'All right. I'll make some tea and you can tell us.'

With their drinks and their chairs arranged near Jeffries' bunk, he propped himself up with pillows and began his telling of a tale. He was enjoying having the audience of three nurses: Beth, Flora and Clara. It was better medicine than anything else he had received that day. In better days, his charm would have enraptured Flora and perhaps even Clara. Here, with him in his pyjamas, he was less of an attraction and more of a diversion with his stories and tall tales.

'It was raining when I woke in the middle of last night,' Jeffries began. 'I thought it was water from the sky, but we were being pelted by gunfire and the spray of grit and mud that fell on the roof of our shelter like a downpour.' He described the curtain of rain, flashing silver like needles in the bursts of harsh explosive light, through which he could see distant men running, falling, splaying. German fire was knocking them down in the middle of the night.

'You should be a poet,' said Beth.

'I think there's enough of them about already,' he replied.

Jeffries would like to have told them that he pulled his boots on quickly in his story, but the truth is that they all slept in their boots, fully clothed. They all knew this. Beth asked him to get to the point. His point was that, as damp and cold as his toes were inside the extra socks his mother had sent, they needed the warmth and protection always. He had seen rats get to men's toes quicker than the frostbite ever would. He stumbled out of his bunk, dragging his pal Charlie Evans from his shelf. They had their rifles and headed through the tunnel, ankle deep in running mud.

When Evans and Jeffries got to the ladder, their hands slipping on the muddy rungs, they paused, waiting to hear orders. Were they to go over the top again, or poke their heads out, rifles raised, ready to shoot randomly at whatever figure ran towards them? Amidst the mist and smoke and rain, it was not always easy to tell friend from enemy. There was shouting all around them. One of the voices was his Sergeant Mills. He could not hear him properly over the din, but Evans nudged Jeffries and nodded upwards. They had to go.

He took a breath. If he thought it would do any good, he would have said a quick prayer that he would get back safe. 'But if prayers did any good,' he said as an aside, 'we would not have been in this hell in the first place.' Something zinged over his head as he climbed over the top of the ladder. By instinct, he ducked down, still looking forward. Evans was with him, his rifle at shoulder height as he stepped into the open field.

'This paints a picture, but I don't see any phantoms in your story,' Beth scoffed.

Flora nudged her with a frown. 'Do continue, Private Jeffries,' Flora said.

In Jeffries' story, the ground was rutted and torn. It was brown, black, and run with red in places that were soft and sucked on his boots. It was hard going. Ahead of the men, the mist was thick with smoke thrown up from shells crashing. It was hard to tell who was who. Those men, Jeffries' friends, blurred alongside the enemy. He thought he saw limbs colliding, bayonets puncturing torsos, and bodies flailing, but the air grew thicker and thicker around them, gradually turning from grey to a sickly yellow.

He scrabbled for his gas mask, tearing open buckles and straps to pull it on. Evans was too slow, his eyes bulging as his tongue swelled and he fell to the bloody mud, clutching his throat. Jeffries was afraid to admit that he had no idea what to do. He could not leave Evans to die, his eyes staring into his, so he gulped as much air as he could and pulled off his mask. He must have thought that he could take in a few lungfuls then he could snatch it back from Evans, but as soon as his mask was off his face, the gas was upon him. His eyes fogged, his face burned from the gas or from the effort of holding his breath. He could not know.

The next thing Jeffries knew, he was beside Evans on the ground, mud surging between his fingers, blood or snot or heaven knows what pouring from his nose or mouth or eyes. He could no longer tell. And then something was on his face. Cold. And he could breathe again.

'When I awoke, the sun was streaming through a gap in the clouds,' he said. 'I was lying on a stretcher, looking up at the lightening sky. Others were milling about, carrying the dead away and the dying and moaning into tents. A nurse rushed past me; her apron spattered with blood.'

'Was that me?' Beth interrupted.

He frowned. 'Possibly. I didn't notice.'

Beth looked put out and sipped at her tea. Clara tried hard to suppress a smirk.

'Standing over me was another private, same as me, but taller and built like a garden wall. Even in the middle of all this blood and mud and snot, he was cleanly shaven, his hair slicked back, and a freshly lit cigarette dangling from his lips,' he continued. 'I asked him if he had another one of them. He passed me a fag, barely noticing me. I said thank you, and he struck a match to get me started.'

Jeffries seemed to think about things for a bit. 'What happened?' Flora said at last.

'Gas attack. I tried to help my pal by sharing my mask but both of us nearly copped it instead. Good thing he was there,' he said.

'Who? The handsome stranger?'

'Well, I was grateful. Didn't think I'd seen him before. I said to him, no disrespect, but you don't sound like one of us enlisted men. You got the looks and voice of an officer. He said he decided to sign up. He said his father and him did not always see eye to eye. Besides, he said, I thought if I am going to be an officer one day, I should start on the ground. See what it's like. What I said was, one way to see what death is like, that's for sure.'

'This is not a ghost story,' said Beth.

'Well, that morning, when we visited the medical tent on the back lines, for we had to administer some disgusting mixture on to our burns, we encountered another man who was not from either regiment. We had been lucky; the gas had barely got to us before we were masked, and fortunately I was covered well, but a blister on my neck needed treating.'

'Another man?' Beth was interested again now.

'Lying on a stretcher in the far corner was a man who seemed to me to be mad. He was raving on about all kinds of madness. He went mostly unheeded, despite his uniform. He wore a battle-stained uniform, although his regimental badges were missing. As I said, he was ignored by most of us until he started muttering about pale figures in the mist, with glowing eyes and teeth that glinted in the darkness. My other new friend – the one you said was handsome - started at this and went over to the strange man. Other duties called me elsewhere, and I left them together, talking. An hour passed before I saw them again, running through grey rain, sprays of dirt and grit falling through the air as a shell exploded just yards from them. They were going in the opposite direction to the rest of us.'

Jeffries went on to describe the new stranger, a man in his thirties, clad as if he had stepped straight out of a shell-hole, laid on a stretcher in a medical tent, recovering from a head wound that he claimed he sustained when he fell against a wooden post. Officers had spent some time questioning the stranger. Giving up, for they were getting no sense out of him, they had left him under armed guard. As the guard was Archie Perkins, with whom Jeffries had shared his cigarette ration when Perkins' ration was eaten by rats, he wandered over. He would give Jeffries no information, but it was then that the stranger stood, straightened his collar, secured the bandage about his head, and buttoned his waistcoat purposefully. He strode off. Perkins, instructed as he was to guard the stranger and watch his every move, sighed with reluctance but followed him anyway. Jeffries took his rifle and followed the stranger and Perkins to the edge of No-Man's Land, pelted by debris and rain.

Rain descended like a sheet of nails, piercing the air, and carrying with it the sharpest of stones, grit, dirt, and chits of bone thrown up by an explosion a mere few yards away. Beyond the noise, Jeffries dimly heard what he thought was Evans' voice calling out a warning. Having thrown themselves to the ground, Perkins and Jeffries crawled to safety.

Clouds of smoke billowed toward them, shielding their view from that of their fellows, and indeed the enemy. Cracks of rifle fire and indistinct voices formed a curtain of sound beyond the smoke. The stranger seemed to wander into the smoke and disappear from sight.

By now, even Clara had started listening, and Beth and Flora were rapt. 'Was that it? Did he vanish?' Flora said.

Jeffries shook his head. 'I looked up into the smoke,' he said. 'There were at least three figures, wider than any German, their outline was threadbare through that sort of veil of smoke. Their eyes glowed. They were harsh points of light. I couldn't see properly through the gauze of smoke. It billowed over us, and my eyes stung whatever it was in the air. I couldn't see, but I heard Perkins' rifle go off and he screamed. I fired into the smoke. When the smoke thinned out and we were just left with the rain, Perkins and those two strangers were gone. It sounds too fantastical to be true, I know, but if it is true, I think they were taken by ghosts.'

Flora and Beth stared at him for a moment. 'What utter nonsense,' Clara said. She got up and took the cocoa cups off to be washed.

'Well, that was certainly interesting. You weave a good tale,' said Flora, brushing herself down as she stood.

'You're missing my point,' said Jeffries, more serious again. 'Except for Perkins, I think they were all ghosts, and the two strangers had to be fetched back. Out there, it's like none of us are alive or dead. It's like we're all in between.' He grabbed her sleeve, tugging on the cloth like a child wanting his mother's attention. 'I dream that they are coming back for me.'

Jeffries suddenly became very tired, and Beth helped rearrange his pillow and straighten his blanket to ease his discomfort. 'I will keep an eye out for them. Between us, Flora and I will fend them off,' she said, softly, with as much warmth as she could. Jeffries smiled thinly and soon closed his eyes.

Later that night, Jeffries died suddenly and quietly. Busy elsewhere, none of the nurses noticed until he had been gone for several minutes. He had simply stopped breathing, with no drama and no noise. He died alone, with Taylor meanwhile raging at empty air, blaming the dirty Hun for all his pain. Later, Taylor was taken away for surgery. It had been decided that the leg was best gone. Taylor had not returned to his bunk when night turned into morning, and Beth had taken her seat beside Private Henson, her kindness a stone cast in a pond, rippling quietly.

THE MINES OF ARRAS

Private William Coverdale had written to his fledgling new wife on the night of 8th April. He had followed his father down the mine at Woolley Colliery, where the great black hills of Wakefield in Yorkshire rolled down to the village of Darton. William was barely twenty years old and was courting Caroline Rathmell when the word came. Ever since Lord Derby had introduced the Group Scheme – what became known as the Derby Scheme – in the autumn of 1915, it was inevitable. And, of course, as the country grew short of men, conscription increased the inevitability of being sent to France.

Derby, as Director-General of Recruiting, pushed for the Military Service Act, which Parliament passed in January 1916. The men who worked down the mines, their days full of darkness and their lungs coated with coal dust, thought they were safe from conscription. The mines would be needed. Some signed up, of course, but William was a homebody. He had never travelled further than Barnsley market. He was relatively safe, being in one of the reserved occupations, but even William was not immune to the flattery of the recruiting officer.

William had met Caroline the summer before. A baker's daughter, she sometimes cycled around the village with deliveries and they had caught each other's eye. He gave her the news at the top of Churchfield Lane, amid the falling blossom of spring. It was April 1916, and the sun was sighing a relieved afternoon as they sat on the wall outside the fishmonger's.

'How was the delving today?' she asked, tugging on her hat as a sudden uplift sought to push it away.

'Early shift, so I was flagging early on. Glad to be by you now, though,' William replied.

He was toying with an envelope between his fingers. She glanced down, not eager to see it or to touch it, but immediately her smiled dropped. 'Something to tell me?' she asked. Her brightness belied glistening eyes.

'Hell fire,' he replied, looking away. 'Lass, I...'

'Is that the Derby letter?' she said, nodding towards the paper.

'Not exactly. The recruiting officer's been round again. While they need us miners here, they also need miners... there.'

'Where?'

'France.'

'What for?'

'Tunnels and that.'

'Oh, aye?' She looked away now. Caroline watched as the blossom drifted down, a stray petal landing in her lap.

'Aye.'

'I knew there was summat. How do you feel about thissen?' She still avoided his eye.

William's fingers brushed the back of her hand. She allowed his fingers to slip between hers and she squeezed tight. 'It's my duty,' he said, quietly, but in a way that made her see how definite it was and how much it would define him. 'There are others going…'

'You can't be the one left behind. I understand,' she said, turning back to meet his gaze.

'It's not…'

'I know.' She squeezed his hand again. 'You'd better get on with it, then.'

'What?'

'Go on.'

'What?'

'Say it.'

'What?'

'Ask me to marry you,' she laughed gently.

He blushed but asked the question anyway. When he thought about it afterwards, he genuinely could not remember whether he had planned to ask her before that moment or not, but when he asked the question there was no doubt in his mind that it was the right thing to do. She hugged him, they kissed, not caring which gossiping passers-by might be watching, then went to tell first her parents, then his. None of them were surprised and none of them opposed it. All was set.

They married three days before William shipped out. They said their goodbyes in private, over two days when they failed to emerge from the bedroom except to eat.

William Coverdale joined the Royal Engineers as a miner, carving out tunnels and quarries underground, alongside tunnellers from New Zealand. Teams worked day and night, in competition with each other, in long shifts, to excavate connecting tunnels. Within a few months, their tunnelling had given rise to a subterranean town, complete with sleeping and living quarters, a church and a hospital. Eight feet high and half as wide, the tunnels were dug at a rate of a hundred yards per day. It became William's job to help fit the anti-gas doors at the end of each tunnel, which was better than when he was sent to disinfect the latrines.

The tunnellers amused themselves by daubing their own signage on the rough-hewn white rock walls. The New Zealanders named their quarries after towns that they knew, so to get his bearings William often had to follow the arrows towards Auckland and Wellington, the latter's latrine particularly pungent. Kitchens and hospital bays were close together so that they could take advantage of the fresh water piped through, but the latrines were sometimes at the end of a steep staircase so that they could be as close as possible to an entrance and some form of ventilation.

In November 1916, on latrine duty, William followed the sign, painted in straight letters with boot blacking, towards the exit that read 'Rue St Quentin, Water'. As he reached the end of the tunnel, he was faced with a junction. One side led up a set up rough steps to 'Men's Latrine'. The other led down a dark, dank corridor to the 'Officer's Latrine'. Although the facilities were separated out, the officers did not enjoy more salubrious means of relieving themselves than the rest of the men. Each latrine was laid out in rows, each row offering a couple of dozen places. 'Place' was the best euphemism they could come up with. Holes had been carved out in the rock, into which the men did what they needed to. Nobody enjoyed being sent to slop them out, but eventually it came to be William's turn.

William humped the barrel of disinfectant on his back, judging it better that any spill take place behind him rather than down his shirt and trousers. It was some sort of lime and chlorinate concoction that smelled almost as bad as the urine and faeces he was sent to use it to wash out.

'Hygiene my arse,' he muttered to himself.

That evening, nobody would sit beside him until he had queued for his shower ration and scrubbed the smell out of his skin. It took several days for it to fade from his clothes, however.

Sleeping quarters were bunks made from several wooden pallets nailed together, and each regiment had a central area where the men could play cards or write to loved ones in the evenings, using empty ammunition boxes as makeshift desks. Chewing on his cooling stew and hunk of bread, William borrowed a pencil and took out some paper he had kept folded in his coat. It was April, two days before the push, and two days before Easter. His thoughts were on Caroline more than usual, and he decided to set out his thoughts to her in case he would not get another chance.

William had known all too well that there were men who had died with the names of their sweethearts and mothers on their lips, breathing their last regret that they still had words unsaid. He was going to say everything as best he could.

'Dearest Caroline,' he began, and crossed it out. 'My Dear Wife,' he restarted, then stopped. Nothing was right.

'Caroline,' he resumed, settling for simplicity, 'I am writing to you sitting on a tea chest. I'm drinking tea that tastes a bit of chlorine. Sometimes it's the only way to make sure the water is clean enough to drink. It was my job today to clean out the latrines, so all I can smell anyway is chlorine. At least it's better than what I had to clean out. The smell is enough to make you faint. But not you. You're made of hardier stuff.

'We have been living like moles here. My days involve digging and carving walls and tunnels. I always have a pickaxe in hand, so much so that it feels odd to hold something as light as a pencil. The boys are in good spirits around me. Johnny Bennett is laughing so hard that it is echoing around the caves like a haunting. Some of the men have painted pictures of their sweethearts on the walls, which brightens the place up. My drawing skills are not up to much, so it is a good thing that I have such a bonny picture of you in my head.

60

'Today I managed to have a hot meal. It was a meat stew, although it was getting cold by the time I could sit down with it. Food has been not bad, although we did complain because the New Zealanders seem to have better rations than us. We all work just as hard, but I suppose we should just put up with what we are given. Jack Jenkins got into a fight with one of the New Zealand boys over a tin of bully beef, but the Sergeant let him off with a warning. Tempers do get a bit hot in these cold caves.

'Sometimes, when most of us are sleeping, we hear distant sounds. I like to imagine that the end of one of the tunnels opens out on the Yorkshire hills, and I can hear the whistle calling the miners home. It is a bit of comfort because I can pretend that I am coming home to you. I hope I will soon, but we are getting ready for something important.

'I will go to bed soon, wrapped up in my coat. As we have dug out caverns with no corners, there is always a draught, so we are always cold. We have some electric light, though, which is how I am able to write to you. The caves go on for miles, and some of the ceilings are as high as a cathedral. We will be having a Sunday service tomorrow, so it will at least feel like we are in church. The last time I was in a church, it was with you, walking down the aisle. I hope that we will walk together again soon in the Yorkshire air instead of the stifling atmosphere that we have down here"..'

He hesitated, uncertain how to sign off. In the end, he settled just for 'Bill"..' He folded the paper and stored it for later. He would keep writing and always carry the most recent letter with him into battle so that it would be on him if anyone needed to check his pockets later. The letters would find their way to Caroline somehow.

The echoes were deep and dark, like bells in a chamber at the bottom of a well. No resonance, no space, no light in the sound. Just distant ghosts of voices and tools finding purchase and grip but slipping, slipping down into the depth of nothing. The faraway phantoms were the New Zealanders, hammering away, tunnelling communications channels and tunnels through these rough-hewn quarries that had lain unused for centuries. Vaulted ceilings of white, chalky stone spiralled their faint echoes to where the British Tunnellers lay. Their beds were bunks made from nailing together wooden pallets, set up in alcoves here and there. An upturned barrel served as a table, tea chests as chairs. The New Zealand Tunnellers were working day and night in eight-hour shifts. The British were in reserve as the Antipodean moles made squared walls and floors of the mediaeval labyrinth.

The tunnels worked through the earth to connect the vaulted quarries were nearly seven feet high and just under four feet wide; big enough for armed and kitted men to march through or to carry equipment. The New Zealand Tunnellers were still going now, in the dead of night, competing to dig ninety to a hundred yards every day. It was the job of the British tunnellers to go behind them afterwards and fit anti-gas doors and an explosive charge. If the Germans ever discovered them, they could be blocked off. That, of course, would leave everyone trapped, like the loyal servants in a Pharaoh's tomb, condemned to be sealed shut in a pyramid to suffocate a long, dark death.

William Coverdale laid awake most of the night, listening to the shadows of sound that haunted the stone, tunnellers seemingly calling up ancient voices from the stone's quiet memories. He wondered how many of the other twenty-four thousand men sequestered in these underground networks were lying awake thinking the same thing. They were organised just like camps anywhere else. Each regiment had its own quarry; Coverdale's was in the Wellington quarry, dominated by the New Zealanders, who named every passageway after parts of their homeland. The nearest command centre was marked out with an arrow daubed on the porridge-textured wall, pointing to Auckland and Wellington. It was at least a way for everyone to get their bearings. At each turn, pillars were given numbers, but giving each cave a name helped the men feel centred in some sort of world. This was important as they slept and woke in a never-ending claustrophobic night.

Sunday morning came, although the morning, afternoon and evening were no different from the night in those gloomy caverns. William pulled on his boots and ran a comb through his hair. He did this several times, each time picking out fewer and fewer lice. He crushed each one under his thumbnail and flicked it along the cavern floor.

Nothing had changed much since he had arrived in that rubble-strewn town square. Hit by repeated shelling, so many of the once-proud mediaeval buildings teetered on the brink of collapse and those that stood undeterred bore the marks of bullets streaking across their facades and pillars eaten away by stray gunfire. New arrivals from New Zealand, including Maori troops, tattooed and aloof, mingled with the fresh recruits from Yorkshire and the Royal Engineers. They had quickly been apprised of their mission, which was to work deep underground to unite the three existing networks of caves, quarries, and tunnels, most of which had lain unused for hundreds of years. William still imagined the spirits of those mediaeval tunnellers haunted the walls, suffused into the stone, to guide the Tommies and Anzacs through the rock.

A staircase from a townhouse cellar hewn from the white clay was William's first glimpse of what would be his subterranean home for the next few months. Laden with kit and carrying a pickaxe, he noticed that territory was clearly marked on the wall. Like dogs emptying their bladders against the trunks of trees, this was the men marking out their territory, and woe betide anyone who questioned it. He followed the others from the rough stairs in the direction of the sign that read '173 miles to London this way'. As if by digging they could escape across the English Channel to the land of tea and cricket. The next set of signs had an arrow pointing downwards for Wellington, and another arrow pointing in the direction of a dark corridor that sported one word: latrine. William would become disappointingly familiar with the latrines during the first few weeks. That is, until his shifts came with the digging team, hacking away at unyielding clay and rock.

The facilities for the men in these tunnels under Arras resembled a small town. There were what passed for bedrooms, communication posts, meeting areas, a medical centre, kitchens and, sometimes, a makeshift bathroom with water boiled alongside the pots in the kitchens. And, above it all, vaulted ceilings looked down in haughty oppression on the men who toiled away like moles. Those from William's Yorkshire regiment were set to work straight away, shifting, hefting, moving coils of wire for lighting and trollies full of rubble in and out of narrow, half-hewn corridors where they had to stoop, hunched like Snow White's dwarves. It was in those first couple of days that he met Johnny Bennett, the joker, and Jack Jenkins, a seething ball of anger and justice who cursed his way through every shift.

The New Zealand tunnellers were sinewy, muscular men drawn from the quarries and mines of a quite different environment from the hellish coal caverns of Yorkshire. Jenkins took an immediate dislike to every single one of them on sight. In fact, even before he saw most of them, he had decided. 'Bastards,' was the muttered refrain as he carried equipment back and forth.

In the oppressive air and depressive temperatures of the caverns during the winter of the closing weeks of 1916, Jenkins and William were laying electrical cable along passageways, securing them to the white clay and wiring them to bulbs, when the New Zealanders caught some of the worst of the angry Yorkshireman's ire.

Sweating and grimy, Jenkins dumped a wheelbarrow of lumps and chippings from a connecting tunnel at the junction between the regions they nominated as Auckland and Wellington. 'Bastards,' he murmured, slightly more loudly than usual. William, hooking lamps to the wall, sighed, hands up in the air. 'What have they done now, Jenks?'

'Bastards. Just look at them. It's like they're allus at it, looking all full of shit. And I'm all bogeyed, can barely keep moving,' he replied, somehow finding enough energy to gesticulate and stab his forefinger back down the corridor.

'Aye, but beefin' about it don't fettle nothing, does it?'

Jenkins glared at him; his cheeks were red up to his eyes. 'Bastards,' he repeated, before he shuffled back down the corridor to pick up the next load, muttering away to himself. The New Zealanders carried on oblivious, whistling, laughing, working the rock harder than anyone William had ever seen. He knew his turn would come, but for the moment he was happy to be useful, clearing up and making those basic facilities a little less basic.

Basic their facilities may have been, but all the men had to work at such close quarters that conflict was inevitable, especially when some of the Yorkshiremen such as Jenkins grew jealous of the preferential treatment that the New Zealanders were getting.

When what was arbitrarily designated as the evening came around in the underground gloom where neither moonlight nor sunlight ever ventured, the men squeezed on benches made from planks and boxes at tables made from splintered doors for dinner. Rations began to transform into something resembling a meal that steamed and smelled of wet washing, whilst the men waited, sitting cheek by jowl.

William sat with Jenkins and his other compatriot, Johnny Bennett, all Yorkshiremen signed up as engineers and miners. Jenkins was eyeing the New Zealanders, who were sitting at an adjacent table, at right angles to bunks that were constructed from old pallets. Coats, kit, and helmets hung from nails haphazardly hammered into the supporting posts. A sandy-haired tunneller sat laughing with another New Zealander with eyebrows that stood out like caterpillars and fingers just as black from a day's picking at rocks. They were passing around a large tin of bully beef, forking out chunks onto their plates already laden with cheese and spoons abrim with stew. It was a hearty meal – hardly gourmet fare but hearty all the same.

Jenkins looked down forlornly as his dixie pan swimming in watery brown food and his lukewarm cup of tea with no milk.

'Bastards,' he said, slapping his meal with a spoon.

'What now, Jenks?' William said, his patience as thin as the stew.

'Look at them. And look at their bloody faces. They get more rations than us, and what do they do to deserve it? Swanning about, taking all the best work and there's us, flagging with nobbut half a plate of whatever this is.'

Not for the first time, Jenkins seemed to be spoiling for a fight. 'Not again,' William warned him through gritted teeth. 'You'll be up for a court martial this time. Don't be starting nowt. You won't be able to finish it.'

'Aye? I'll finish them bastards, no trouble.' The volume of his voice was rising now as he leaned back in his chair. He wanted them to hear.

William put his hands up. 'Don't say I didn't warn you.' Beside him, Johnny Bennett laughed, but this time his humour was hollow. 'Do what you like, Jenkins, but you'll be on your own.'

'Aye, might have known you'd step back. Full of big words with your jokes and your laughs, but that's all for nowt when you need it. All mouth and no trousers.'

Johnny's smile dropped. 'Be as stoddy as you like. You won't be winding me up to join you in any court martial. This stew's good enough for me.' Johnny turned to his food and shovelled in a brown lump of something that resembled meat. He winced. Whatever it tasted of, it wasn't beef.

Behind Jenkins, the New Zealanders shared a joke all their own, laughing and banging the table with their spoons. To Jenkins, this was as if they were taunting him. 'Bastards!' he exploded.

The one with the eyebrows turned, amused by Jenkins' outburst. 'What was that, pal?' he said.

Jenkins rose from the bench, his tea in his hand. 'You heard me.'

'Thought I did. We done something to annoy you, Lord Teacup of Englandshire?'

'Aye,' replied Jenkins. He relaxed into the coming conflict. The name-calling had given him an opening, so he tossed the tea, now grown cold, in the face of the one with the eyebrows. Fists flew, benches kicked askew. Johnny Bennett took his plate into a corner to finish on his own, and William ducked out of range of elbows and knuckles. Other men quickly swarmed around Jenkins, pulling him back, forming a barrier between him and Eyebrow Man. He waggled his caterpillars in mock disappointment and turned back to his food. Jenkins was dragged off to a quiet corner.

Later, on his way to the latrine with a bucket, William came upon Jenkins hunched in a hollow, staring at a stalagmite and smoking. Involuntarily, William coughed. With scant ventilation, cigarette smoke had quickly lost its appeal. Jenkins glared up at him.

'So, I'm the bastard now, am I?' William said.

'No. I just…' He stared into the little hollow between walls.

William put down the heavy bucket, taking care not to spill anything. 'You just what?'

Not looking at him, he simply replied, 'I just want to go home.'

'Where's home?'

'Wakefield.'

'Ah. I'm from Darton, near Barnsley. Not far from you. We could've been down the same pit if things was different.'

'Well, we're in this pit instead.'

'We are. Hell above, hell below. Could be worse.'

A distant hum of voices, deep and warm, united in a hymn, drifted down the quarry. 'What's that?' asked Jenkins.

'That way is cellar 5E. Battery Headquarters. The chapel. There's a chaplain down there holding the Sunday service.'

'You going?' Jenkins peered down the dark avenue towards the sound.

'I'm on piss and shit duty. Didn't you notice? Got a bucket of dirty water from the kitchen to chuck down the latrine. No church for me. Maybe some other time.'

'Aye. Maybe.'

That night, whilst others snored in their bunks, including Jenkins and jovial Johnny, William took out his pencil and wrote again to his Caroline for as long as the light from stump of candle that he had would allow him to. He once again related the story of Jenkins and his fighting, and how he narrowly escaped a court martial by the strength in numbers of Yorkshiremen who banded together to keep him from trouble. He filled her in on how, by and large, the Anzac soldiers were hated for their casual attitude, their hogging of the rations, and their reluctance to salute British officers. But they had to rub up against them day after day, week after week.

And those weeks turned into months. Months of digging, months of carving out tunnels and passageways to link up the quarry networks to provide secret underground routes for men to wait until the signal came to surge above ground and attack the German front line.

Finally, in April 1917, the push was coming, and the time now came for Jenkins and William to finally consider gracing the chapel with their presence. William's letter to Caroline that afternoon was clear. 'I have to think that these might be the last words I write to you,' he wrote, 'as I know what we have facing us is a big push. The boys have been saying that it is more like winter than spring up there. It is April, but there is rain and frost on the ground, which will make it very unpleasant for us. I suppose that the Germans will suffer too. One thing will keep me warm, and that is thinking of you. If I die with that thought in my head, it will not be a bad death.'

William Coverdale's home in Darton was high up by Woolley Colliery, where a long road swept from the village to rows of farm-workers' cottages that were repurposed for the pit. Up there on the hill, the slag heap stood like a mouldering hunchback that sweated the odour of dank, woody earth. Still, when the sun rose, feeling its way along the rooftops, its magic lit the darkest corners of his heart.

Now, on Easter Sunday in the catacombs of Arras, the fist of darkness held his heart firm and cold. Men hunched over, toiling to carve angles from heaps of jutting rock. Their only homes were bunks built from discarded planks; their village green an upturned tea chest. The smells were of ammonia, stale sweat and, drifting in with each morning, cordite.

The walls around him merged into the floors and ceilings, still rough-hewn and white but adorned here and there with the hastily daubed directions and imperatives. The kitchens and medical centres were close to each other, signs identifying where water points and latrines could be found as far apart from each other as practical. Close by, one sign read 'No spitting allowed'. Water for drinking was boiled or chlorinated, with a half measure of lime thrown in to destroy any tiny bugs. William preferred to boil it himself and bypass the chlorine if he could. The most overpowering smell, though, was Cresyl, the disinfectant that was used to clean the latrines. On his depressingly frequent latrine duties, the phenol lingered in his nostrils even after his shift was over.

March 1917 had seen the completion of the underground work, where William had worked to lay the lighting, tunnelling channels through which pipes could bring the air they needed to not suffocate. Spanning at least twelve miles as far as Wancourt, the underground network was fed by the rail lines that he also helped lay in narrow passages where the walls could not be widened. There were advantages to being wiry and lean, after all.

Organised like military camps, twenty-four thousand men were poised, ready to launch an onslaught against the German frontline. Embedded as they were just a few miles away and above their underground enemy, the German army had terrible weapons at their disposal: poisonous gas and the deadly flamethrower that they had already used against Russia to horrible effect. In William's cavern, his brigade was billeted in the various side caves; all four thousand of them.

On the afternoon of 8th April, before the Easter service, it was William's job, along with dozens of others, to clear the tunnels in his brigade's section of any debris so that departure from the caverns would be unimpeded at zero hour. The mixture of trepidation and excitement that suffused the atmosphere, laid in by the murmuring of men in corners. Truth be told, although William thought of them as corners, they were merely dips and curves and alcoves. The lack of any real corners meant that draughts always swept through with the speed and ruthlessness of an evil ghost. This day, men huddled, smoking, preparing; waiting, waiting, waiting for what would come with the dawn.

The immensity of some of the walls, sweeping up above like the roof of a cathedral, offered a blank canvas. Graffiti adorned many walls. William stopped at one wall. The lines scratched on the wall with pencil, ink or blade were as if the artists had scraped the skin from the inside of their souls and laid it bare on the rock. No graffiti criticised or mocked senior officers; most of them were portraits of their own sweethearts left at home, a way to connect their underground lives to the sunrise over their own hilltops.

William ran his fingers over the undulating stone, the chalk worn smooth by dozens of men doing the same as they drew their loved ones. Some inscriptions were more votive or religious. Crosses accompanied biblical quotations, and one read 'Thanks be to God for this shelter from shells and bullets.' William smiled at the irony of being billeted in the bowels of the earth, so close to hell, but still the faith could be found to thank God for it. There was no God down here, he noted. An older drawing, preserved since 1914, depicted Charlie Chaplin, and some talented waggish cartoonist had scrawled the character Krazy Kat from the comic papers. The caricatured feline was shown leaping, as if going over the top to join the fray.

William's eyes rested on rested on two sketches, side by side. One, signed by a Private Frank Deaney, was accompanied by his date of enlistment and his regiment, and was a crude, simple outline of his wife. Lines showed the curve of her lips, the shape of her eyes, the flow of her hair. William had no idea who he was; he had passed through, gone on somewhere else. Was this his goodbye note or his testament to a love he would never see again? The other sketch was astonishingly accomplished. It was unsigned. The woman was drawn from a lower angle, her head slightly to one side, her eyes lost in shadow, her hat framing her face. Her lips were downturned but not with sadness. The characteristic curvature of her top lip was well observed by an artist who had lingered over that face many times in his life and, now, in his memory and that of the thousands of men who passed by.

William poised his hand, with a lump of charcoal that he had obtained from supplies, hesitant, about to trace the lines of Caroline's face on a bare spot of wall. He closed his eyes, searching for her face in his memory. There were snatches: he could delineate her chin, her lips, the incline of her nose; but each time he focused on one feature, the rest blurred away, as if misted over behind a window on a cold day.

'Oh my God. I'm forgetting her,' he said to himself. He flung the charcoal to the ground and walked away.

The months of drilling, digging and explosion after explosion to clear sections of quarry were coming to an end. In

November, William's team had struggled to get anywhere near the target of a hundred yards in a day, despite shovelling pound after pound of gravel into sacks and then into wagons. A town's worth of limestone and chalk yielded to their pickaxes. By Christmas, they were knocking through five hundred yards in a week; two thousand yards by the end of December, when seven quarries were finally connected and electrical cables drawn through. They lived in this subterranean town of transmission posts, dormitories, kitchens, and even its own hospital, Thompson's Cave. Rails carried wagons full of rubble, ammunition and, sometimes, the wounded themselves. This vast labyrinth could not have been more secure, with entrances guarded by a manmade Cerberus of retractable airlocks and booby traps. No one undesirable could possibly get in. The biggest challenge would now be in getting out, where their tunnels would emerge in No Man's Land.

In the largest cavern in their quarry, William's regiment crowded into the space. With hats and helmets in hand and heads bowed, they listened to the chaplain as he intoned words of comfort. A table was pushed up against the central column of white stone beneath the sign pointing to 'Batt. HQ'. A pair of candlesticks were arranged either side of a cross and a small bowl, a tiny votive that offered very little except the men's prayers.

Jenkins and Johnny Bennett lined up with William. The men were closely packed in rows. The vaulted ceiling echoed with their voices as they repeated the words directed by the chaplain, resplendent in his white cassock. His back was to the men as he intoned, facing the table as if it were an altar.

Johnny Bennett stifled an initial snigger, but soon went into silence, his eyes downcast, lost in his own thoughts during the service. Jenkins glanced around, seemingly suppressing seething anger, his lips pressed close together. For William, the Easter service was a matter of enormous indifference, but the sound of hundreds of men lined up in the cavern and along the tunnels, each one repeating a ritual prayer, mesmerised him. The voices, deep and solemn, spiralled up into the high chamber, as if becoming part of the ceiling above.

The chaplain began with his address, 'Jesus Christ, risen master and triumphant Lord', ending his verses with 'In your mercy, forgive us.' Each repetition of this was followed by the men repeating 'Lord hear us and help us.' William's eyes went to the ceiling, where the cavern tapered to a dark nape that swallowed the end of each echo. They declared their faith, the ritual repetition of 'Christ died for our sins' seeming to be an empty gesture from this dank hole in the ground. The Lord's Prayer followed, which every man knew by heart.

'The peace of the Lord be always with you,' finished the chaplain.

'And also with you,' came the chorus.

Quietly, Johnny Bennett mouthed the word 'bollocks.'

Some men clutched bibles Bibles close to their chests or stood reading passages to themselves. Most took the time to talk together, even wishing each other a Happy Easter; some with irony, some without. To William, it all seemed empty, meaningless. He believed in God he supposed, but what did that mean here? What did prayer bring them that luck, strategy, or their wits would not?

At the chaplain's signal, the men dispersed, and separate queues for each regiment formed. 'What are we queuing for now?' sighed Bennett.

'Rum ration,' William replied.

'Fair enough. That'll do me.'

With tin cups in hand, each soldier took a dribbled measure of black, slick rum from a stoneware jug poured by one of the privates who doled out rations each day. It was warm going down, filling William with some momentary confidence, as if it were some kind of elixir that would see them through. It was more likely just to see them through some fitful sleep without too much complaining.

As the men laid in their makeshift bunks that night, where dusk and dawn saw no division, they stared at the ceilings, their eyes boring into the rock that hung under the floors of cellars, under farmer's fields, under the hopes and fears of the men, women and children of Arras who prayed to be delivered from relentless destruction of their homes and lives.

Above, as it had since the day of attack had been fixed, bombs fell, wave after wave, on enemy ground. Four days of shells flooded the land, a barrage designed to distract the Germans from the coming surprise emergence from deep underground. Deep in the caverns, dull shuddering rocked the ceilings, an echo of the explosions on the ground above. They were in the stomach of a whale assailed by a terrible storm. Unknown to William, gas attacks ravaged other men through the night.

William dreamed of Caroline. More than a sketch in his sleep, she swept with the breeze at the door of their cottage. He slept with her smile and woke with a calmness that belied the day ahead.

Thousands of troops were lined up in short order along the caverns and corridors of chalk and darkness, their exits just a few yards short of the German front line. Johnny Bennet whispered a silent prayer; Jenkins glared with determination; William kept the dream of Caroline in his mind as they waited in that early dawn of Easter Monday.

William helped carry the explosives to the top of each stairway, ready to blast their exit into the freezing morning air. At a little after five in the morning, the signal was given for an explosion that would have deafened Hades himself, on his throne in the underworld. All men lined up, close enough to hear each other breathe, helmets tipped over their eyes, bayonets held straight up like a staff. Ferociously, the head of each tunnel exploded, belching forth the underground men, troglodytes suddenly transformed into a pack of wolves. Marching towards the light and smoke, they gushed into German territory, vomited from the guts of the earth.

A mile or so away, a dense curtain of fire gave cover for the regiments from the tunnels of Arras to push forward. William was behind the first and second waves, a cacophony of smoke and rattling, battering noise enveloping him. He followed bellowed orders along with Johnny Bennett and Jenkins. The orders were to start digging a communication trench between lines to link to a stretch of the old German front line that would be used as a stage from which to dig into the current German front line. It was a hastily put together plan, and a dozen men set to work digging the short stretch of shallow trench. It would provide cover for moving forward, but it left them exposed whilst they dug. William had never before been more dependent on the shield of his pals.

They had managed to dig down about six inches into the cold, frosted ground with shell fire a constant backdrop. William told himself the attack must be going well. He dared not look up; just keep digging into the earth. His spade hit a rock, skidded to one side. He lost his hold on the handle and it slapped to the ground. As he leaned in to pick it up, a boot bore down on the handle.

William looked up. The owner of the boot was an officer, the brutish Captain Villiers, a blustering blister of a man with red cheeks and an enormous moustache that he styled after Field Marshal Douglas Haig. He seemed to imagine himself more in command of the war than he actually was.

Villiers barked at William, 'Look alive, Sapper! Dig! If you can't dig, then get down to that line and take a German bullet!'

Blushing, William would not meet his eye but waited until he moved his foot to the side. He picked up the spade and renewed his efforts. As one, the digging party uncovered earth and stones, digging down and down.

As they reached a foot down, a rifle shot split the air so close by that William's hand instinctively clamped hard on his ear to shield it from damage. Captain Villiers' weight brushed William's leg as he pitched forward, landing face down in the trench. A fresh bullet hole was dribbling white gore and blood from the side of his skull.

The diggers all grabbed their rifles, abandoning their spades.

'We need to see where that shot come from. Somewhere the other side of that line of trees,' said Johnny, pointing. The men quickly split into two groups: one went left; the other skirted right with William.

The land dipped down behind the trees, at right angles to the advancing line of attack. William threw himself on to his stomach, rifle under his chin, scanning for tell-tale signs of disturbance in the earth. A miner would know. He quickly got a sense of void over the mound on which the trees stood. 'I think there's a deep dugout down there,' he said.

Jenkins was beside him, looking hard. 'I can't see it.'

'Trust me. There's cover there that's facing the wrong way. Branches of a hedge that are facing backwards. Just compare it to the trees. See?' Jenkins squinted. He nodded, although only William could really see. 'There's someone in there, just fired out and hit the Captain. Sitting still now, waiting to see if we've spotted them.'

There was movement in the foliage. Jenkins was on his feet. He fired into the hidden dugout. In an explosion of leaves and twigs, a German private spilled out, staggering, clutching his throat. He fell, quickly still. William and Jenkins joined the others as they surrounded the dugout, looking down on the remaining two Germans, crouched in the hole, arms raised in surrender.

The left-hand party opened fire as one. After a moment, they all returned to their digging.

A shell landed next to a team manning a Lewis gun as William's group passed them on the outskirts of the village of St Laurent Blangy. A cloud of debris and dust burst between them, and the men dissipated, seeking visibility. As if wading through fog, William lost track of his companions. Coughing khaki blurs moved through the billowing dirt towards distant cottages.

Head down, William pressed on through the thickening mud as the rain intensified: hard and sharp and cold like needles. There had been firing but he could see no enemy ahead; perhaps it had come from behind. He turned, wiped the water from his eyes just as the wind gusted the rain against his side. Through the dirty chainmail of rain, he could see two German soldiers climbing out of a camouflaged dugout, now firing at the backs of the rest of his team. One man fell, caught with a bullet in his back, and was swallowed up by the mud. Intense fire was returned. In the melee, through the icy rain, it was impossible to see who was who and which was which. He could only stand and watch, not knowing where to aim.

As the rain paused and the view began to clear, William thought he could see Jenkins, but there was something odd about his gait. He was walking, but there was something lopsided. The fingers of his right hand were trailing along the ground, his rifle discarded. William blinked. Jenkins' arm was a length of skin, loosely connecting shards of bone. From opposite directions, dodging stray barbed wire, Johnny Bennett and William ran to Jenkins' side. Johnny took him gently and laid him down. His pack on his back provided a sort of seat that enabled him to sit up. He was delirious, mumbling something through dribbling lips as his mess of an arm tangled within itself by his side.

Johnny turned to William. He was the most serious that William had ever seen him, his face ashen in the driving wind and rain. 'Can you hold him down?' he said.

'Aye. What are you thinking?'

Johnny produced his jack knife, unsheathed. 'His arm... it's just hanging by a string. If I make it as neat as I can, we tie him off with a tourniquet.' William nodded and held Jenkins by his shoulders. If Jenkins screamed, it was drowned out by the storm of gunfire and the renewed volley of rain.

With the tourniquet tied, Johnny gave Jenkins his canteen and grabbed William by the arm, pushing him on. 'Go. There's a gap through there – follow the others,' he said, pointing. Stunned, mute, William obeyed. He had gone just a few yards when the next shell landed behind him. He looked back. Jenkins and Johnny were laid across each other, both limp and soft as butter.

Blinking through the rain, William left behind all thoughts with his pals and joined the next wave laden with heavy packs, facing into a morning of metal and murder.

MISSILES

My family came here when our nation was youthful and full of hope. Everything seemed balanced. All kinds of foreign businesses were here, investing in infrastructure, building roads, houses; more businesses. Government was focused on efficient and productive education and healthcare systems: the best life we could achieve for all of us. We felt as if we were the chosen people. Like all good things in life, though, it came at a cost. This is our land, there can be doubt. We were displaced by history many centuries ago, and others had settled here, built their own cities full of their own ways that were not ours and, we believed, defiled the land that was bequeathed to us. When history turned full circle and it was time for us to be resettled in our homeland, they had to move. History shows that we have the right, and that their tenancy was only ever going to be temporary. You cannot blame those who lacked our education for not knowing and for reacting so badly to resettlement. Their leaders have to carry the blame for what followed. Years of bloodshed, people fighting for possession of land that they knew was not theirs to fight over but ours. Years of them defying our will and provoking us into war.

I joined the army when I was seventeen, happy to sign up to do my duty. Initially unsure, I was swayed by the images of them in their concrete shacks, firing rockets from home-made emplacements, surrounded by their laughing children, at our land. The stories of young soldiers lost to this war and their weeping mothers and girlfriends did not stop me. I signed up to train for what I do now.

I sit at a bank of screens, controller in hand, a calibrated joystick that precisely identifies targets. We have our satellites and drones that bring us pictures of where they hide, and the buildings in which to plan their attacks, store their weapons and make their bombs. Some of them masquerade as schools or hospitals, and each time we strike, they parade injured women and children in front of the cameras to make it seem as if we are deliberately killing their families. My orders are clear: I am not to zoom in any closer than to verify the shape of the building and its structural weaknesses, then press the button – more like a trigger on my joystick – that sends our missiles to the targets. We are almost always successful. But that doesn't stop the international media relaying their images of murdered children. We are not murdering children. We are targeting munitions and terrorists to protect ourselves.

This time, I have decided to prove it, if only to myself. It is against orders, but I tell myself it will be understood once I can share the recording with my commanding officer. I calibrate the software to show the highest magnification and zoom in as I send the missile towards a street on their side of the divide. On the face of it, this seems to be a residential area, but our intelligence tells us that it hides an entrance to an underground bomb-making facility.

We have given warning. The siren sounds. People run. Not just women and children – the terrorists too. The missile comes closer. The whine as it descends through the air must be deafening. The impact is slightly off-target, taking away the side of a neighbouring building as well as the roof of the facility. I watch longer than I should. Instead of reporting success straight away, I wait. I wait for the dust to clear. Through my grainy video image on the bank of screens before me, I see rubble. I see twisted metal that may be girders, or rocket launchers. It is hard to tell. Torn fabric shows me that one of them was simply a curtain pole. Lying under the metal and amongst the rubble are bodies. I count at least twelve, none of them moving, some in strange positions. They are all small, short people. Children.

I scan the recording, the live image, all the data, carefully. There may be weapons there, but I have missed them. I have killed children. This building was a legitimate target. We have the right. But this is out of balance. I had thought the propaganda that we were killing children was a lie. I was wrong. Thousands of their civilians dead, ours only in single figures. Dozens of our soldiers killed in the line of fire, as many of their terrorists as we can find. But their terrorists look the same as their civilians on my screens. I cannot tell. Things are out of balance.

I send the data back up the line to my superiors. They seem content with my work. Nothing is questioned. The live feed is still showing on one of the screens. I cannot hear, but there is screaming, weeping, anger. But also there are people wandering amongst the rubble retrieving belongings. No one seems to be searching for weapons. One man picks up a teddy bear, holds it to his chest. A child sits on a lump of concrete, alone, crying. A man seemingly around my age looks up. He cannot possibly see the camera from where he is, but he seems to be looking into the lens from this massive distance. I wonder what he is thinking. No, I know what he is thinking.

When the order comes to send another missile to the same target, to make sure we achieve our objective, I hesitate. There is no longer any doubt that civilians would be hurt, and if we are slightly off-target again, will we try a third time? And a fourth? This is not balanced.

The order comes again. I calibrate the system. I make sure the missile launcher is armed. I set the coordinates. They are not the same coordinates I was given. This time, the outcome might be more balanced.

BITS

It was the third time I had caught the train to London in my life. The first time, I was a young bride-to-be, on my way to shop for wedding dresses with Marilyn. She was my bridesmaid. We were both in bits, we were so excited. The second time, my husband had treated me to a theatre weekend. He chose Starlight Express. We never went again.

This time, I was going to visit my son. He didn't seem much older than the two boys sitting across from me. They had a table in the carriage and were facing each other. Both had a sort of Turkish look about them, all dark hair and London accents. The thin one wore a washed-out tee shirt. His spiky elbows looked cold. His haircut was all close cropped and his features were pointed as if there was barely any skin on him, let alone fat. His companion made up for it a bit, chunky and huddled in his hooded top. His mound of curly hair made me jealous: I've never been able to curl mine very well. He had a little straggly would-be beard. It was like it needed plucking rather than shaving, poor boy. He stared absently at his mobile phone screen as his thin friend jabbered away. I did say they reminded me of my son. That was, of course, until they started speaking.

The carriage was empty apart from the three of us. I sat reading my book, in my twinset and pearls, with my straight old hair. I could have moved up the carriage but that would have been impolite, and politeness is so important. Outside, the blur of the world sped by.

"Round about here we was stopped last time," said the thin one to his friend.

"Here?" the other one replied, not looking up from his phone.

The thin one jabbed a finger at the window. "Yeah, Levent. Here".

"Here?"

"Yeah!"

"Yeah?"

So. Levent was his name. Turkish, I think. I was right. I have an eye for where people are from. When Gladys moved in next door, the hairs went up on the back of my neck before she even spoke. I could tell from the look of her she was from Birmingham, and when she spoke it was confirmed. I wouldn't mind, but that accent is so grating.

We thundered through a level crossing, cars queued at the gate, waiting for us to speed past. The lights were flashing at the point where the thin boy was pointing.

"It was this man, right," he continued. "He stepped out into the road as the train went past".

"In the road?"

"Yeah, and we had to stop, right?"

"But the road..." Levent was smirking at his friend, still looking at the glowing screen on his phone.

"The track, man. The track!" replied the thin one, throwing his bony arms up in the air. "He stepped out and I heard the crack! Right here was where we had to stop. Police, ambulance, the whole lot".

Not precisely 'right here', it must be said. The train had moved on quite quickly, clattering away into the countryside. But still, my interest was piqued. I had to keep listening. I stared at the words in my book but they were just pictures to me. My concentration was somewhere else, with these boys.

"Yeah?" acknowledged Levent.

His thing friend leaned on the table, waving his pointy finger about as if to prove he was telling the truth. "Yeah, we had to wait while they, like, were... picking up his bits. I think," he said.

Sometimes, one overhears the most unusual conversations in train carriages. I imagined the scene that he was talking about: a body in bits carried away piled up on a stretcher; ambulance men and police milling about in yellow visibility jackets; flashing lights from their cars strobing the night through the cold pouring rain. The thought was strangely comforting.

"That's the job to have though," said Levent.

"What, picking up bits?" said his bony friend.

"Nah, train driver. You don't even have to turn or nothing. Straight line, that's it. Just keep the train on the - um - straight line. Thirty-five grand a year. Thirty-five K for doing nothing!"

"Thirty-five is crap though".

"I wouldn't sniff at it".

My son was a student doctor. Briefly, I wondered what these boys would grow up to be. Tax accountants, maybe? 'Big Brother' contestants? Prisoners? Neither of them could have been more than twenty, perhaps twenty-two years old. I flinched a little, although I didn't want to. I wasn't used to being on trains, which is ironic, given my late husband's penchant for train-spotting.

The boys were still talking. My attention had wandered, but I tuned back in to their chatter. I couldn't help it. The thin, pointed one was talking again, spreading his hands wide to show he was telling the truth.

"She was saying 'I honestly want him to stop but I couldn't stop him or do nothing'. When I'm with my boys, that's when I do it. Skunk. Weed," he said.

"Things is, Erol, this is the age when you shoudn't," replied Levent. At last, his name. The bony one was called Erol, and now he was proving they were far from the potential lawyers, doctors or accountants that I wondered. Every time I give these types the benefit of the doubt, they show their true colours sooner or later. I buried my head in my book, but I could feel my cheeks burning red and the muscles around my lips tighten.

Erol boasted, "Last week at a party I had four glasses of Bells and Coke, three WKDs, three Jack Daniels, and the next day I had this much Smirnoff". He measured several inches high off the table with his hands. "And I tell you, man, I was sleeping on the floor. I didn't know where I was".

I thought so. Scum in the making. Just like my husband. He used to drink. And drink. And drink. Sometimes he didn't know what he was doing either. My hands were trembling. I put my book down. It was no use pretending I was reading it any longer. I reached into my handbag for what I needed to steady my nerves.

Erol was in the middle of another tall tale. "...and then I slapped him, like that," he said. "Then I called my boys, but I said, nah. But then I had to deal with his bits".

I stood up, rummaging in my bag. I crossed the aisle with a step. I was talking to those greasy youths before I realised it. "My late husband enjoyed slapping people too," I said. "Me in particular".

Then the hammer was in my hand, and I continued, "At least, he did until I knocked him on the head... and he staggered into the path of an oncoming train".

Whiskery Levent looked up with mild surprise. I don't think he fully registered what I was saying until the hammer made the first dent in the side of his head. Bony Erol started screaming right away, his fingers clawing at his sallow face in girlish terror. He was in bits. One strike in the middle of his forehead, a neat hole the size of a ten pence piece, and he was done. Levent made a mess of the table top when the blood started to well up and spill. I broke his nose and smashed his teeth. He was soon silent, staring into space instead of his screen.

I looked down at the grubbiness. Without noticing, I had trod blood into the carpet.

"Oh dear. What a mess," I said to nobody in particular.

MONEY

"Good morning," chimes the voice in the phone. "Welcome to MidWest Bank. If you are a customer, please enter your sort code and account number".

I obey. "If you require information about balances and withdrawals, press 'one'. To open another account, press 'two'. To enquire about an existing complaint or register a new one, press 'three'..." I stop listening to the details. I just want to know how I can get to speak to a person, or what passes for a person in some automated call centre in Glasgow or Bombay or wherever it is. "...customer service advisor, press 'zero'". I press. I wait.

"You are in a queue. Your call is important to us." The voice thanks me for my patience; then it plays me a tinny panpipe version of *Wind Beneath My Wings*.

While I wait, I lean against the brushed steel rail. The food court is behind me, busy with shoppers, the escalator below. I could really do without having to phone the bank on my mobile in the middle of a shopping mall. I could just go to the nearest branch – there's one on the floor below – but by the time I've queued only to be told I need an appointment, I might as well stand here looking spare. Besides, I have another reason for not going. There might be people I know working there. I am shivering. I really wish I'd worn a coat, but, well, I don't have one. This jumper has to do. I could put on another layer but I need two hands to do that and it would be just my luck to get through at that exact moment. I wish I could buy a hands-free kit.

"Hello, MidWest Bank, how can I help you?" It's a Scottish accent, possibly Edinburgh, and quite friendly. I tell her my problem. She takes my account number, sort code, security number and my mother's maiden name, and then puts me on hold. Maybe I didn't give enough information. Blood type needed, maybe?

Another voice in another department interrupts the wispy panpipes of *My Heart Will Go On*. I explain again. "I applied for a credit card almost two months ago. I sent in the forms, and since then I've heard nothing".

"Yes Madam, let me look at your details on the screen." This involves forty-five seconds of static silence. "I can see here that your application has not progressed since 21st April."

"I think I just told you that. I'm calling to find out why."

"I don't know. I'll have to transfer you to the relevant department…"

I have to resist the temptation to throw the phone down towards Tie Rack. "No, hang on. Can't you tell me anything?"

"I can see that you were sent a letter on 11th May. Have you received that?"

"Letter? No. What does it say?"

"I can't tell you that. It's confidential information."

"But it's addressed to me, and you've just verified who I am. Emma Green".

The voice, disembodied and dispassionate, ignores my rising frustration. I feel my own voice reaching squealing level. I swear I'll stamp on this handset in a minute. I should know better, but I'm feeling desperate. "I can send you another letter, Miss Green."

I've lost. I could let off some steam into the phone but I'd only get a pre-programmed response and probably look pretty undignified in front of dozens of strangers. "Do that, then."

"Can I help you with anything else?"

"No thanks." I hang up; thrust the handset into my pocket. I look around; I suppose to check whether anyone had been listening. No, everyone has better things to do. None of the countless people going about their own business even notice me.

I lean forward on the rail, looking over the edge at the people standing patiently on the escalators, moving between layers of shops, boutiques, cafes and more people. So many are clutching bags splashed with the names of chain stores. How do they all afford it? They've all got credit cards, that's how. Until payday, I can't even buy myself lunch.

My foot kicks against the black bin bag at my feet. It bulges with old clothes. My gift to Oxfam or whichever charity shop will take it. I had sat down, once I had put Tom to bed, and gone through the wardrobe. I tried to slide the wire hangers along the rail but it was too full. Spilling the clothes onto the floor, I was searching for anything new-looking enough to put up on EBay, but it seemed so thin, cheap and washed out. Like me. So I bagged it up, brought the bag with me.

I slide down the barrier and sit beside the bag. I clutch it on my lap, like a teddy bear. I think of Tom when I do this, biting my lip. I have no idea what to do next. My other three credit cards are at maximum. I can transfer at least one of them to another zero per cent interest rate for a few months when it finally comes through, but in the meantime I've still got to make this month's payments. The monthly bills are going out by direct debit in the next couple of days, including the electricity, the rent and repayments on the two loans. Yesterday, I went to pick up the phone to "consolidate" my debts into "one convenient monthly payment", but then I realised I had already let BT disconnect me. I survive on the mobile, with the pay-as-you-go. Most people ring me. Most of my friends and Mum know how hard it's been for me and Tom, managing on our own, without The Bastard. Mum calls him that now as well. It's kind of funny. Except it isn't.

I had met Darren at work, at the bank. Midwest. How ironic is that? Not the one in this shopping mall, mind you, another one. We were both behind the counter, young (well, youngish) and enjoying life, such as it was, with no responsibility and no chains. He was confident, good-looking in a cheeky sort of way, and I was probably an easy target: quiet, not a party girl, but slim and pretty and, to be honest, grateful for the attention. He scooped me up, moved me in, got me pregnant, then moved out. It wasn't that simple I suppose, but it felt that quick. I couldn't keep working after Tom was born. It was too much, on my own. I went into the bank one day to try to see him, to show him what he'd walked away from, but the word was that he'd taken a transfer to another branch. In a way, it's a pity. He's got a beautiful son that he'll never know anything about. In another way, he's a total and utter bastard and I want to stick hot knitting needles in his eyes.

I'm not really very comfortable, sitting on the cold, hard floor. My knees, tucked up to the bag, are starting to ache. I stretch my legs out to help the muscles back into a more comfortable shape. As I do this, the tip of a bulbous white trainer glances over my scuffed shoe. It isn't that exactly that makes the teenager trip, though, it's the fact that a stray thread from the frayed hem of his dragging jeans catches my toe. He trips, skids, falls on his knee. He swears as the lid of his tub-sized industrially thick milkshake clips off and the contents spill down his hand. His friends laugh through their baseball caps as he blushes through his spots. Embarrassed and angry, he sees me getting up, trying to apologise. Or maybe he just sees red.

Half of the milkshake lands on my chest, a lump dropping to my lap. The remainder hits the polished floor. I don't react, I just look. He looks back for a moment, then runs towards the escalator with his friends. Other people also look, but they have their own concerns and look away, suddenly interested in a shop window or their fingernails.

I'm lucky that I have a change of clothes with me. As furtively as I can with half the shopping centre regarding me

105

with a mixture of suspicion and sympathy, I jump the queue for the ladies' toilets. They can all see the state of me: no one argues. In the cubicle, I tear open the black bin liner. I sift through the old t shirts and threadbare jeans and pull out the warmest thing I can find. I peel off the milk-caked clothes that I am wearing and pull on an old musty, bobbly half-zip fleece and a pair of cheap supermarket jeans, dark blue with a knee-sized hole in one leg. I stuff everything else back in what is left of the bin bag, but I can barely hold it together.

On my way to the exit, outside the bank, the ripped bin liner finally gives up and empties its guts onto the floor. On my hands and knees, I gather it all together: some clothes a picture of who I am now, some a faded reminder of what I once had. One is even an old hat that I bought on a whim and wore once. I leave it upturned and, tired, I sit with my back against the glass of the bank's display window, my head below a sign offering fixed rate mortgages.

My eyes are closed when I hear the first tinkle of coins. I look. Someone has dropped two ten pence pieces and two five pence coins in the hat. Whoever it was has moved on.

Then there is someone else. A man, six feet tall, slightly chubby but good-looking in a cheeky way, drops a pound coin and a handful of coppers in the hat, seemingly his change from buying the Marks and Spencer chicken salad wrap that he is holding in his other hand. He winks at me as he chomps down on it, then walks into the bank.

Transferred.

He doesn't recognise me.

Maybe I'll go in.

THE SELKIE WEDDING

It was the day I lost my brother. It was a day of high winds and roaring rain. It was a day I'll never forget, but it isn't where this story begins. This story is the story of me growing up, and it begins on a sunny day.

I came home from school one day in June. I was in Year Seven, so I was getting close to the end of my first year in secondary school. I was feeling quite pleased with myself. I had just made it into the football team, and practice had gone well. Liam Atkinson had given Harry Stevens a wicked sliding tackle that sent him flying. Mister Hickie blew the whistle and sent them off, which was fair enough seeing as Harry had kneed Liam in the thigh as retaliation for the tackle. That was the best dead leg I'd ever seen. Not that I approve of that sort of thing, but it was even cooler than that time I picked up that handful of hair from that older girl round by the music block. That was a wicked fight, two of them tearing hair out in the playground. I gave it to one of the teachers.

It was one of those rare days when I had remembered to take my door key to school, so I let myself in through the back door. Our back door steps straight into the kitchen, so it was handy for dumping dirty football boots outside and tumbling muddy kit into the washing machine. My shorts had a big grass skid on them, so they went in. My shirt and socks were OK but they smelt like Dad's armpits so I bundled them in too. I was just about to put the powder in the drawer and switch the machine on when I heard a noise from the next room.

Mum wasn't usually home from work yet, so the little hairs on the back of my neck stood to attention. I could hear drawers being dragged open and the insides of them shaken about. Someone was looking for something. There was the rattle of pens and keys and what Mum calls 'bits and bobs'. There was the ruffle of paper and the slap of things being put on top of the sideboard. Someone was in the sitting room.

I tiptoed into the hall. The sitting room was just a few steps around to the right. I didn't know what I would do if I did find a burglar in there, but in a way I was too scared not to look. My heart was beating so hard that I could feel it all the way up in my head. The door was ajar. I could just see the corner of the sideboard, and papers scattered on the floor. Some of them were piled up on the sideboard, so they must have fallen off.

As I got closer, I heard a voice: a sigh and a quiet "For God's sake, where is it?"

I opened the door. "Hello, Mum," I said.

She half looked up at me as she pulled out a drawer full of old ordnance survey maps that Dad used to use when he went hill walking.

"Mum?"

"Yes, Jamie?" she said, not looking up.

"Why are you home so early?"

She started leafing through the maps, all folded up and dog-eared. "Oh. Um, I'll tell you in a minute. I have to find something. Did you have a nice day at school?"

There was an old, torn-open envelope sticking out from between the folds of a map. It caught her eye and she took it out. She didn't seem to hear me at all.

"It was okay," I said. "Aidan Young got a detention for flicking bogeys at Samantha Bird. I had football practice after school."

Mum took a piece of paper out of the envelope and sat on the edge of the sofa, reading it.

"I said I had *football practice*, Mum," I said.

Mum was concentrating. "Really? Oh, was it good?"

"Alright," I shrugged. "What's that?"

Mum crumpled the paper back into the envelope, and crammed the whole thing into her pocket. "I'll tell you in a minute. What do you want for tea?"

"I'll tell you *in a minute*," I said, heading back into the kitchen.

We had spaghetti out of a tin, with sausages (which I ended up grilling myself) and a couple of potato waffles that Mum found in the fridge. She hadn't gone shopping on the way home from work, which she usually does. As I poked at my food, I realised that Mum hadn't even been in her suit from the office when I got home. She was wearing her weekend jeans and an old top.

"Mum…"

"Jamie," she said with a mouthful of waffle.

"Did you actually *go* to work today, Mum?"

I could tell that she thought for a moment about not telling me the truth, but it had been just Mum and me for so long that we didn't do that anymore. Not about important things.

"Well," she said, putting her fork down. "I was on my way out of the door when Bill came up the drive." Bill was the postman: short-sighted, a granddad twice over. Not Mum's type. "He had this letter," she continued, pointing to an envelope next to the ketchup bottle on the table. I hadn't noticed it before. We both looked at it. Nobody touched it.

"Don't you want to know what it is?"

Well, duh. "Suppose so."

"It's an invitation to a wedding."

"Oh," I said. I shovelled half a sausage. It wasn't anything important, then. I expected it to be from some distant cousin or friend of Mum's.

"I had to check something," she said, "but it took me ages. I was in a bit of a panic, actually, because I couldn't find it. I spent most of the day checking your Dad's boxes in the garage and in the loft, and then it was in the sitting room drawer all along. Serves me right for not sorting it all out sooner. But, you know, I couldn't really bring myself to do it."

"I know, Mum," I said. Don't start now Mum, please. I never know what to do when you get going with the tears. "What was it? The thing in the drawer, I mean."

She pulled the crumpled envelope from her pocket, straightened it out, and stood it against the sauce bottle. The other envelope lay at its feet. Suddenly, I noticed that they were both addressed to me. *Me.* Jamie McCormack. That's not right. I'm too young to get mail.

"You've been invited to your brother's wedding," she said. "I had an address to reply to the invitation, but that was the bride's parents. I had to find your brother's address and phone number. Since he… since… um…"

I stopped eating. "You mean, since Dad died and Callum stopped talking to us, you didn't think you'd need his address and phone number ever again?"

"Something like that," she said quietly. See? No lying.

I suppose that, in a way, this was where me growing up sort of started. I saw a side of my Mum that I hadn't seen before, or maybe I had seen it before but never noticed until now. She could have kept the whole thing from me, but she didn't. She wanted me to know. She wanted me to decide. Mum handed me both letters and I opened them.

The first one was from Callum, and was dated two years ago, a few weeks after he left. It read:

Dear Jamie,

Your still my brother. Carol and me might of had are ups and downs but I wont forget you. Here is my address and phone number…

Apart from the amazing spelling, this was like Callum leaping out from the past. I hadn't seen or heard from him since he left. 'Carol' was Mum. Callum called her 'Carol' because she wasn't his mother. *His* mother died before I was born - *my* mother was Dad's second wife. To begin with, Callum and Mum got on fine, especially when I came along. When I was little, it seemed to me that Mum treated us both the same. I didn't find out that she wasn't his mum too until Dad died. Then suddenly it was like a war zone in the house. At the time, I didn't really understand what they argued about or why he left, but he never came back and Mum never spoke about him. Until now.

I opened the other envelope. Inside was a rectangular card, cream-coloured with the letters raised and shiny. There was a pattern in the paper that felt bumpy when I ran my fingers over it. The spelling on this one was perfect, inviting me plus one guest to the wedding of *Callum Gordon McCormack and Isla Mary Finn at the Banqueting Hall of Eilean Donan Castle on Loch Duich.* You've probably worked out by now that my and Callum's Dad was Scottish. Callum's mother was Irish, and mine is English. I don't know if there are any Welsh people in the family.

"Where's Loch Doo-itch?" I asked Mum.

"I think it's more like 'Doo-ick', Jamie. It's in the Scottish Highlands."

"Wicked. I mean, I didn't know that's where Callum went."

"Last I knew, he went to be a fisherman in Orkney."

"Where's that?"

"Even more north than Scotland." We live in Norfolk.

"Wicked. Bet it's cold."

"Yes," she said. "You'd better take a coat."

* *   *

The Loch Duich Hotel is in the Highlands, as Mum said. The area was wet, windswept and very Scottish. You can get there by air, landing at Inverness Airport. You can also arrive by train. Both of these would have been quicker than driving by car, which we did. By 'we' I mean Mum and me. She got me out of bed in what felt like the middle of the night, and we set off. We stopped at service stations for toilet and food breaks, but otherwise it was non-stop. It was dark when we arrived, and we checked in to the hotel straight away. We got a 'family room', which meant that Mum had a double bed and I had a single bed over the other side of the room. It was all frills and net curtains, like Grandma's room in the nursing home. It was all that Mum could afford. I wasn't complaining, as Callum hadn't even invited her.

Mum's plan was to get me to the wedding, then spend the day walking along the loch and over the hills, like Dad used to do. But we had a couple of days until the wedding, during which time I was meant to get to know my brother again. He was coming to pick me up from the hotel the following morning.

The hotel was white and long, with hills rising behind and 'Loch Duich Hotel' spelt out in flowers along a bank in front. Mum said it was 'quaint'. That's not the word I would have used to describe it. The Eilean Donan Castle wasn't far away from the hotel, on a little island at a point where three lochs meet. The scenery spread out like great octopus hands of water, liquid fingers snaking around ancient stone ruins and the occasional farmhouse or hotel. The castle looked as if it was growing out of the rock, held in place by the watery hands. I almost thought it might float away on its own at any moment.

In the morning, I had breakfast with Mum then waited outside for Callum. I sat on a little low wall at the edge of the car park, kicking my heels against the brick. It was September now, and although the sun was shining, the wind whipped about so I needed my coat, a big padded thing that I zipped up to my chin. My baseball cap didn't cover my ears so they were a bit stingy from the morning cold. But I didn't mind. I was about to meet my big brother for the first time in two years.

Coming in from over the hills, a man came up to me with his dog. It was a big wiry mongrel with fur like steel wool. He was old, with a gingery white beard, a thick overcoat and a woolly bobble hat. The man, that is, not the dog. He said something that I thought was 'good morning' but I hadn't quite tuned in to the Scottish accent yet that morning, so I wasn't sure.

"Alright," I said, trying not to encourage him.

"Laddie," he said.

I tried to pretend I was looking at something in the distance, which in a way I was. I was waiting for Callum to arrive.

"You staying in the hotel?" he asked, leaning against the wall. His dog sniffed at my trainers.

"Yeah. With my... with my family. They know I'm here. They're probably watching."

"Aye."

The dog looked up at me. Without thinking, I patted its head.

"He likes you, laddie. Mind you, that dog likes everyone. Trusting soul. Have you been here before?"

I looked at him. He had a dog. Mum wasn't far away. Callum would be here in a minute. I decided I could talk to him. "No," I said.

"Ah, then you won't know much about the area then."

"Not really. I'm just up for a sort of holiday."

"We're very famous for seals up the water a way. Otters, fresh fish and seals."

"Seals? I thought they were only, like, in the Arctic or something."

"Aw no, laddie. They live in and around the lochs. Lots of them. Or selkies, as we called them when I was a boy."

"Selkies?"

"Aye. Old Orkney word for seal. But selkies were something else too, way back in time. You've not heard the legends, then?"

"Uh… no." I should have said yes. He's going to tell me a story now. That's *all* I need.

"Och, well then. There are many tales about the Selkie Folk, and they go back hundreds of years. They're wee gentle creatures who can change from seals into bonny people. They come ashore at night and dance on lonely moonlit beaches. Some say they'd do it once a year at Midsummer's Eve, some say every ninth night. They would shed their sealskin to change into people and put it back on again to change back."

Images of slinky seal-women dancing in the moonlight swam around in my head. "What happened if they lost their skin?" I asked.

There was a twinkle in the old man's eye. "Och, if the sealskin was lost or stolen, the selkie wouldn't be able too change back. There are many stories of men stealing a lassie selkie's skin and making her his wife. These tales usually end in tears. Like most marriages!"

The old man amused himself with that and chuckled away for a minute. I peeked at my watch. Callum wasn't late yet.

"Legend has it that there's a ghostly bearded man who wanders the hills around the castle calling for his lost selkie love who found her skin and returned to the sea. If you listen hard, you can hear the wind carry his words, calling her name."

I shivered. But that was because it was cold. Honest.

The man patted his thigh, calling the dog to his side. "Enjoy your stay," he said with a wink, "and don't go chasing after any selkie maidens."

"Okay."

"Maybe see you in the bar tonight, laddie. Name's Angus," he said as he set off down the bank with his dog trotting on ahead.

"I'm Jamie," I said, but I don't think he heard me.

I could tell it was Callum a mile off. He drove into the car park in a mud-spattered Land Rover Discovery, and I knew it was him before he pulled up. It wasn't exactly like he was an older version of me: I look too much like Mum. But there was so much of Dad in his face, some of which I've got. I suppose we've got the same sort of nose. I could see that even through the grey-streaked windscreen of the car. Callum had filled out a bit since the last time I saw him, with his rucksack over his shoulder, leaving the house key on the table. It was my key now.

"Jamie-boy!" he called. His window was wound down so I could hear him.

I smiled and ran around to the passenger door. I climbed in with more confidence than I expected. My brother!

"Hello Callum," I said, putting my hand out to shake his. He grabbed it and used it to pull me into a stifling bear hug.

"Jamie! Good to see you!"

I buckled myself in and we set off. Callum asked me about the journey up, and the hotel, and what I thought of Scotland. He didn't ask about Mum.

As we drove along the shoreline, the mist began to roll back over the water, clearing in the heat of the breaking morning. Over on the loch, a grey seal slipped off a rock with a splash. As it swam under the surface, a flipper flicked up. It looked like a salute. Or a wave.

Callum looked like a fisherman, in his big baggy knitted jumper, oily jeans and boots. He had day-old stubble and a mess of curly hair and smiled as if he'd won the lottery, even when he took a sharp bend a bit too fast. He drove like Dad did. Too fast.

"So... you're in high school now then, wee Jamie?" he said.

"Yeah. Secondary school. Year eight now. It's the new term really, but Mum let me have a week off to come up here. For the wedding, y'know."

"Och, yeah! It's ma weddin'! Tae a bonnie wee lassie!"

"That is the most fake Scottish accent ever, Callum. You lived in Norfolk for *years*!" We both laughed. We were back.

"I suppose you want to know all about Isla, then?"

"Well..."

"Cheeky! I'm telling you anyway, wee brother. I was working as a fisherman up in Orkney for a while, but they had to lay a few people off, so I got a job delivering fish to hotels, shops and restaurants along the coast here. I got talking one day to Andy McVitie who owns a café a few miles back that way, and he invited me to his birthday party down on the shoreline. It was an outdoor do in the summer and there she was in the evening, staring out at the loch, in this silk dress and long dark hair. Love at first sight it was."

He grinned at me.

"*I* didn't think she was bad either!" he added with a laugh.

"Do you still deliver fish, then?" I asked.

"Yeah. Not much else available really. But we're doing okay. Isla's an artist. She's a painter – sells her work in local galleries. Mostly watercolours, some oils and stuff. The tourists love them."

"We've done some painting in art, in school. I'm not very good at it. We have to paint old shoes and things that Miss puts on a table in the middle of the room."

"Exciting, eh? Isla does views over the loch, and close studies of the water. You'll see when we get to the cottage, they're beautiful."

We chatted about not much for most of the journey. We compared notes about football. Callum used to support Manchester United, like me, but now he said he supported Glasgow Celtic. I couldn't really understand why except that he seemed to be trying to be properly Scottish like Dad was.

Callum's cottage was in a village further up the shoreline. It was an old stone building with a modern extension. The gravel on the drive crunched under the tyres as we arrived. Isla met us at the door.

Shaded by overhanging branches from a cherry tree in the garden, she at first seemed very shy. Her hair draped smoothly over her shoulders, long strands settling in the wool of her jumper. The bagginess of the jumper couldn't hide the fact that her body curved gracefully like the waves on the loch. Her feet didn't seem to make any sound as she moved over the gravel to my side of the car.

"Hello. You must be Jamie," she said. Her skin was like milk.

"Helloooo?" she repeated.

I blushed. "Oh, sorry. Yeah. Jamie. Hi. I'm Jamie. Nice to meet you, Isla."

Callum and I climbed out the car. He and Isla hugged and held hands as they walked into the house. They showed me around. It was cosy but small. Every wall was hung with her paintings. Some showed the shoreline or the coast at night, some during the day, but most were at sunset or twilight. She had painted some beautiful shapes with the reflections of the sun in the water.

We sat together and had a cup of tea in her workroom, which was a downstairs bedroom cleared of all furniture except an easel, stool and some old chairs. A half-finished canvas stood on the easel. It was all shades of blue and green, a blurry underwater picture of what looked like a seal diving for fish. It was like we were seeing it through murky water.

I liked those paintings, which was kind of funny because I'd never be caught dead talking about the use of light and colour in a picture if I was at school. I'd end up trampled under the dinner queue.

We carried on talking. They told me about the plans for the wedding. There was to be a champagne reception at the castle, where the ceremony would also be performed. I'd never heard of weddings not being done in a church or registry office before; I thought it was the most exotic thing I'd ever heard of. Both Callum and Isla seemed really excited about it.

"Will there be lots of guests?" I asked.

They looked at each other quickly, as if to check something before answering. Callum said, "Not really. There's you and some of our cousins, and Auntie Margaret, Dad's sister. The last time you saw her you were a bairn. We've got a few friends too, they're all coming..."

Isla interrupted gently. "I don't have any family here. They all live very far away and couldn't make the journey. So it's a wee small wedding but that's how Callum wants it."

I wondered if what *she* wanted was the same thing.

A little later, the sun had heated up the day enough for us to go out into the garden. We sat on plastic chairs, drank squash and ate biscuits. Isla went out, walking to the village shops to run a few errands for the wedding. She mentioned the florist and the baker. She was expecting the wedding cake to be ready. Callum's garden was long and thin, the far end snaking around a corner past an overgrown hedge. In front of the hedge was an old shed. I could just glimpse the roof of another shed behind the hedge. Old used wood, some it stripped, some if it with paint flaking, was stacked up by the hedge so that it was difficult to get around to the other shed. The lawn was overgrown. Mum always let me mow the lawn at home; I was the master of the mower.

"I like your garden," I said, sipping my squash.

Callum looked at me for a moment, than laughed. "Cheeky!"

"Maybe I'll mow the lawn for you while I'm here."

"Aye, maybe. Listen…" Here it comes. "How's your mother?"

There was something about the question that I didn't like. "She was *yours* as well for a while," I said.

125

Callum stared into the distance. "My mother died before you were born, Jamie. I'm ten years older than you, remember. I was only a wee bairn when she died, and Dad had to manage on his own. We were doing fine. Then Carol comes along, gets herself pregnant, then Dad had to marry her."

Hang on a minute, I thought. I don't like this. I could feel my face burning, and I couldn't stop myself. "I think Dad had *something* to do with Mum getting pregnant too! He didn't *have to* marry her – I've got loads of friends with Mums and Dads who aren't married!"

It was as if Callum couldn't see how upset I was. Or maybe he didn't care. So why did he invite me to the wedding? In a flash I could remember snatches of arguments between Mum and Callum, like watching a movie trailer in my head. They were always about Mum trying to control his behaviour. He was the kind of teenager who would go out drinking and getting into trouble. Twice the police brought him home late at night. Eventually, he grew out of that but not before he grew to hate my mother – his stepmother. Dad wasn't always around, often working away, so it was left to Mum most of the time. I could see now why he left.

"So why'd you invite me to the wedding if you hate me so much?"

"You're my brother, Jamie. I…" As he struggled with what to say, his mobile phone rang, a shrill noise that pierced the air. He pulled the phone out of his pocket and flicked it open.

"Yeah?" he said. There was a pause while he listened to the person at the other end. "Okay, I'll be there in ten minutes."

I stared at the lawn. Some of the grass was so long that it swayed in a slight breeze.

"I've got to go out for a wee while, Jamie. One of the other drivers has called in sick. I've got to go and pick up the van and make a couple of deliveries. It's extra money, and we could do with that right now. I won't be long, and Isla will be back soon. You'll be fine here, will you not?"

I stared at the grass. "Yeah," I said. "Maybe I'll mow the lawn."

Callum was already concentrating on finding his car keys, patting his pocket and glancing around. "Aye, if you like. It's in the shed. Just don't go in the other one."

"Why not?"

"Because it's not *in* there, you numpty. It's full of old stuff of mine anyway, old things from when I was a kid that I need to sort out. Best left alone for now," he said. He retrieved his keys from a plant pot. He had placed them there when he was getting drinks and biscuits. "Right, I'll be off."

With that, he got into the car, started up the engine and was gone. It seemed like he was using it as an excuse to run away from the conversation. I was alone in someone else's garden. Although that someone else was my brother, I felt uncomfortable sitting there, as if I was trespassing. But I didn't want to upset him any more, so I thought I'd help.

I went into the kitchen and looked for a hook on the wall or a key box. Nothing. There were some drawers. I pulled out the one closest to the back door. In amongst a couple of light bulbs and some of those 'bits and bobs' was a bunch of keys. I took it with me into the garden.

The second key I tried opened the nearest shed. The smell of wood was in the air, floating out of the walls. Stray bits of cobweb fell into my face. I rubbed my nose furiously to get rid of it. There were boxes, cardboard and plastic, with tools and screws and nails in; there was an old bicycle with a wheel missing; and there was a rusty old lawnmower. I had only ever seen this type on TV. It was one of those that you push along, with the blades revolving forward on to the grass, spitting the cuttings out as it goes. No hover mower, no electrical cable, not even a petrol mower. I wouldn't be brave (or stupid) enough to mess about with petrol anyway. I looked at the mower. I could see that it would still go but it would be hard work. There was nothing to collect the grass cuttings unless I emptied out one of the plastic boxes, but how would I scrape it all together anyway? I needed a rake. But there were no other big garden tools in this shed.

I climbed past the loose planks and went round the back of the hedge to look at the other shed. It was a safe bet that there would be a rake in there as there wasn't anything like a spade or fork in the first shed and *everyone* has a spade, surely. So that kind of thing must have been in the other shed. There was that big 'but', though. Callum told me not to go in. But he also said I could cut the grass. I thought about it for what felt like ages. I decided eventually that, if I had the key on the bunch, I'd open the shed, grab a rake if there was one, and close it up again. Callum would be so pleased that I'd got the garden neat and tidy for him that he wouldn't mind. It could be my wedding present for him. I know Mum bought something off some list in a department store, but this would be something from *me*. Something personal. Something to show that we were proper brothers.

I tried all the keys. None of them fit the lock. I thought again. I could still do it, just scoop the cuttings up with my hands and put them in one of the plastic boxes. So I went back and emptied out a dusty tub full of old hinges, bags of screws and loose bits of wood and metal. It had a sticker on it with the handwritten words 'Loose Bits'. The contents tumbled out onto the shed floor. One of the transparent bags of screws had something in it that caught my eye; something mixed up with the screws. It was a key.

*   *   *

The shed behind the hedge was old. The hinges were a little rusty, so it opened stiffly, but the key turned easily in the lock. There was so much stuff in there that it was dark. Broken toasters, an old TV, tins of paint and half-used boxes of tiles were stacked up along one side, blocking part of the window. There were boxes of old magazines and comics on the floor, piled up like breeze blocks. I could see the handles of a few garden tools in the far corner, past the boxes, next to another heap of things covered with an old blanket. It looked like there could be a spade, a hoe, maybe a rake there. There was a gap between the boxes and the TV just wide enough for me to squeeze through sideways. I scraped through, my jeans wiping a layer of dust off the TV screen.

I reached for the rake. It was upside down and its prongs caught on the bottom edge of the blanket as I tugged it away from the tangle of tools. The blanket came with it, sliding off the heap of things underneath. It flopped to the floor heavily in a cloud of dust.

The heap turned out to be an old chest of drawers with some more random junk on top of it. It was then that I had a thought. Callum said there was stuff in there from when he was younger. Maybe there would be pictures of him and Dad from before I was born, maybe even pictures of me. Maybe I'd get to see what Dad's first wife looked like. He had never liked to talk about her, which Callum probably didn't like very much.

I pulled open the biggest of the drawers. It was stuffed with screwed-up newspaper. I rummaged through and soon found that the newspaper was hiding something. A long box that probably originally held boots or wellies lay at the bottom of the drawer. It was quite heavy but I managed to drag it out. There wasn't really enough room to open the box in the shed so I decided to take it outside to have a look. Once I saw what was in there, my plan was to put it back where I found it.

Outside, I lay the box on the grass and knelt beside it. Before I could open it, though, the sunlight on me was suddenly blocked by a shadow. I swallowed a heartbeat. I looked up, expecting Callum to tell me off.

"Hello, Jamie," said Isla. "Where did you find that?"

Isla and I sat at the kitchen table, just staring. We were staring at the contents of the box. I didn't know what it was to start with. It was black, with shades of grey and even cream, all mottled with big dark spots. If I rubbed my hand over it in one direction, it was smooth. My hand glided over it as if it was sliding on ice. But if I moved my hand in the other direction, the sealskin would grip my fingertips and hold on tight. That's right: sealskin. The skin of a seal, all folded up in a box.

I thought of the story that Angus, the man with the dog, told me. Selkies. I stopped staring at the sealskin and looked up at Isla. She was still staring at the sealskin. She was beautiful, her long dark hair pulled back now behind her neck. She wore a t shirt now and I could see the smoothness of the skin on her arms, as if it was new.

"I haven't seen this for a year," she said at last. "Callum told me he had burnt it."

I didn't know what to say.

"When I came ashore and met Callum, it wasn't the first time that I had visited, and I meant to go home again, but there was something about him that I fell in love with. I couldn't help it. We don't hide our feelings well, and we don't shy away from them either. I wanted to stay with Callum as long as I could, so I didn't want to keep anything from him. When I told him, we had already moved in together. He took this skin away. He said he had burnt it. I believed him. I never even thought to look in his shed. So, when he proposed marriage to me, it seemed like the only stream to follow."

I wasn't sure that I understood everything she said. I think now that I just didn't want to understand because the truth was just too weird. But I had to ask.

"Sorry, you said you told him something. What? I mean…"

Isla placed a hand gently on the sealskin and looked suddenly into my eyes. "I think you know, don't you, Jamie? You've heard the stories of the seal-kind who take human form to dance in the moonlight and maybe take a husband or wife, only to return to the water later. There are so many tales."

"What are you going to do?"

She paused, breathing heavily. There were tears in her eyes. I thought at any moment that she would start sobbing, which scared me because I wouldn't know what to do.

"Callum didn't burn this. He wanted to trap me into staying with him, but he loves me enough not to destroy it. But I think he will if he finds out that I have it. He gets so jealous sometimes, even if another man talks to me in the street."

"But –" I began, but I didn't know how to help.

Isla put the lid back on the box and picked it up. She stood by the back door, clutching it to her chest. Tears were streaming down her face now. "Sometimes, in the night, I hear my family calling me."

Then she turned and walked out of the door.

I did my own crying when Callum got back. I had sat at the table, stunned, not knowing what to do or say, for about half an hour. I think that Callum already knew what had happened when he saw that Isla wasn't there. I told him everything. I didn't exactly say which of us found the key and went in and got the sealskin, but between sobs I told him everything she said to me.

My big brother hauled me back into his Land Rover. There was anger in his eyes but he didn't say a word until we were a couple of miles down the road. He sped around corners, his eyes darting along the shoreline, seeking out signs of Isla in any distant cove or rocky outcrop.

"Keep looking!" he said to me.

I did, but it was no good.

Suddenly, Callum slammed his foot on the brake. We skidded to a halt. "I've been so *stupid*," he said, resting his forehead on the steering wheel. "We're going the wrong way!"

"What do you mean?" I said as he turned the car around.

"Andy McVitie. She'll go to where he had his party, back on the beach. But it's miles in the other direction."

Callum gripped the steering wheel like it was a gun that he was afraid to fire. He definitely broke the speed limit driving back the other way. How we didn't end up in a ditch or in water I don't know. We were lucky that there were no other cars coming the opposite way. We had to stop for a moment for some sheep to cross the road, but we roared off again as soon as they passed.

I had already said sorry so many times that it was annoying Callum, but I couldn't stand the silence. "What are you going to do?" I asked.

"Stop her," he said.

"Stop her doing what?"

He didn't answer.

When we got there, we had to leave the car in front of a low wall that looked down on a pebbly beach, washed by the spray from a rough tide. Callum ran ahead, with me lagging behind. He wanted me to stay with the car. In the distance, an arm of rock stretched out over the water. The surface on top was flat. Isla stood there, the sealskin in her arms, flapping in the wind.

Rain started emptying down like buckets of pellets. It was hard and hissing and now I couldn't see Isla clearly at all. Callum ran towards her, stumbling a couple of times on loose pebbles. As he got closer, the harder it seemed to see her. The rain made it difficult to see her shape properly. She seemed to drape the sealskin over her bare shoulders. I blinked the rain out of my eyes, and when I could see her again on that rock, it was a darker shape I saw, lying down, edging closer to the edge.

Callum was on the rock now, slipping and shouting her name, but as he reached out to her, she disappeared off the rock. A wave exploded against the rock, spraying over Callum's head, and she was gone.

I couldn't hear him over the roaring rain, but I could tell he was screaming her name, over and over.

I had to call Mum on Callum's mobile, which he'd left on the dashboard. She had had lunch in the hotel after her hill walk and was having a lie down, but she came and fetched me. Callum was still on the rock, calling to the loch. He barely seemed to notice her at first, but he turned and spoke to her. I was too far away to hear, but I could see him crying and Mum wrapping her arms around him like she used to do with me when I was younger. It was like she was *his* mum too again.

We got him home and Mum helped cancel all the wedding arrangements. I don't know how Callum explained it to all the guests. Maybe he just said that she went out driving and never came back. That's what Mum said when we lost Dad.

I'm in Year Eight now, and still in the football team. I scored the winning goal against our biggest rival last week: kids from a posh school, too scared to slide in the mud. I talk to Callum on the phone sometimes, but he doesn't have much to say and he doesn't come to visit. He still delivers fish, driving up and down and along the lochs, so that he can keep an eye on the shore. Legend has it that a selkie may return to land every ninth day, so he organises his shifts so that he can spend a whole day searching for a splash in the water and the shape of a seal cutting through the waves on the loch.

Some versions of the legend say that a selkie will only return to land on Midsummer's Eve. Maybe Mum and I will go and visit him then, but our lives are moving apart again. That day that Isla slid into the water, a big part of Callum swam away too and never came back. That was the day that I found my brother and lost him at the same time.

ZOMBIE

Hugo Lupin was pronounced dead in August. In November of the following year, I sat in the benefits office with him. I had to prop him in his chair to stop him sliding under the table, and the lady behind the computer wouldn't talk to us until I'd swatted a couple of the flies. A few of them buzzed around his head and a tiny maggot crawled along his left cheek, but I don't think she noticed. His drooling probably distracted her.

"Mister Lupin," she said, "we have no record of you either paying national insurance or actively seeking work for well over a year. Unless you can account for your whereabouts I can't process your claim."

Hugo said, "Wwrrghh".

"What did he say? I don't recognise his accent. Where is he from?" There was more than a hint of contempt in her voice. Really, people doing her job need more patience.

I pulled my chair a bit closer to the table. My thick spectacles started to slip down my nose. I pushed them back up. I wished I could afford better ones. "Well, Lithuania originally," I said, "but that's not the point. As I said before, Hugo hasn't been able to work because he's, well, he's a zombie."

"Immigrant, then. With a disability." I'm not sure she took me literally. "Are you his carer?"

"No. I mean, yes. Sort of. Derek Timmins, that's me. We're friends. Or, we were, at least. He was my best man. But I'm divorced now. Hugo's unmarried."

The benefits lady was obviously thinking something sarcastic. Her lips curled up at the corner, as if she was trying not to smile. Or she might just have been trying not to breathe in the smell.

She said, "I see. Take this form along to the third floor. Ask for Eileen." She handed me a form. It had a long number along the top and lots of boxes to fill in.

"Are you Eileen?" I said to the curly-haired woman behind the counter on the third floor. Her hair was either a bubble perm or an exploded floor mop, I couldn't really tell. She looked at me from behind her copy of *The Daily Mail*. I couldn't help noticing the headline 'Undead scroungers sucking us dry'. I read *The Mirror* myself.

Eileen took the form from me and looked it over. "You're looking to claim benefit... disability... housing. We can't do any of this unless you're looking for work."

I leaned on the counter, trying to gain her confidence. I'm not really any good at this, but I tried laughing as if we're in on the same joke, and rolled my eyes as I jerked my thumb over my shoulder at Hugo. He was drooling behind me in the queue. "Not me," I said. "I'm Derek. It's for Hugo. He's homeless."

"Does he have a visa? A work permit? DNA coded ID card?"

"Well, he *is* a zombie."

She looked at him as his chin rested on my shoulder, his tongue lolling, dribble staining my jumper.

"He looks dead on his feet," she said.

"Like I said."

"Well, we won't see him starve. I see he is staying with you as his sponsor, but he must have a bank account. We can't pay him otherwise."

"Won't he need money to open an account with?"

Her answer was to send us to the bank.

The girl behind the counter in the bank was very young and very smiley. Just a few years ago, I might have tried to ask for a date, but I've become older, fatter and anyway she didn't look the type who would appreciate my *Buffy* collection taking up half the living room.

She smiled so much that her lips barely moved as she said, "You can open an account with as little as a pound. Would you like an overdraft facility? We have zero per cent balance transfer rate on our credit card. Just sign here."

She tried to hand the form to Hugo. He was staring at the lady in the queue who had a Yorkshire Terrier peeping out of her handbag.

"Well, I'll be signing for him," I said.

"Oh, I see," she said, her smile failing. "I'm afraid we don't allow just anyone to have access to the money of those with special needs. We need…"

"But he's a zombie. He's not even a very good one to be truthful. He's never really got the hang of craving human flesh, and his shuffling frankly lacks menace. He just wants to get on with his, y'know… unlife."

She folded her arms, the smile now a scowl, one eyebrow raised accusingly at me. "So he's dead then?" she said. "We'll have to freeze his assets until a relative produces the relevant legal documentation."

I flung my arms wide in desperation. "Well, there's a death certificate. But you see, he's a zombie!"

Then there was a strange combination of sounds. A crunch was followed by a squelch, then a scream. I turned to see Hugo tucking into the lady's Yorkshire Terrier, dog blood spattered all over his dry, flecked face. The lady had fainted to the floor, which was probably a good thing.

"Oh, Hugo! Couldn't you wait? I gave you a rat before we left!" I said, without much effect. This was embarrassing.

The following day, I put Hugo on a lead. It was a dog lead. The old lady didn't need it anymore, so I borrowed it. He choked as I abruptly jerked him back from shuffling after a Jack Russell. It was a windy day, with bits of paper swirling around us. I think someone had dropped a load of fliers in the park instead of delivering them. I did that once when I was a kid, with free papers, instead of hoisting them on my back and delivering them to the council estate. I got found out when they clogged up the canal.

We sat on the bench in the park, watching the wind swirl leaves and paper. "I can't go on making excuses for you, Hugo. Even if we are best mates."

"Ak!"

I had pulled the choke chain again.

"You'll just have to get a…"

I noticed that one of the fliers had landed on his face. Being a zombie, Hugo didn't really have the wit to peel it off.

"…job."

I read the flier. It read as follows: "Stop the exploitation! Burger chain 'King McChicken' employ workers without ID! They only pay half the minimum wage! No unions! No records! No rights! Don't exploit society's victims! They don't want employees who think for themselves!"

It seemed perfect.

A month later, with Christmas not that far off, on a really cold day, I'd just gone through a really weird experience on a bus that got stuck in a tunnel. There was some strange bloke on the bus who persuaded a girl to get off the bus. He was spouting some escaped nutcase stuff about aliens and whatnot. The girl got off the bus. A couple of the passengers went after her but couldn't find her in the tunnel. The driver carried on and, when we got to the station underneath the shopping mall, the loony fella disappeared into the shopping crowds. The whole experience made me feel a bit woozy, and a bit hungry, so I decided to pop in to where Hugo was working to see how he was doing.

King McChicken wasn't very busy. A thin girl who I knew from the *Star Wars* all-nighter at the Odeon, Wendy, was at the till. I looked up at the burger display and menu list. There were a couple of new promotions on the go.

"Hello, Derek. Can I take your order?" said Wendy.

"Yep. I'll have a cheese-rimmed triple bacon rumpburger and fries. How's Hugo doing?"

Hugo shuffled forwards from the kitchen area behind. I hadn't smelled him coming. It must have been because of the grease smell. He looked quite smart in his cap and apron.

"Okay," said Wendy. "He's lasting longer than some others. People just keep disappearing."

"Good. Got a new job myself. Doorman at the wig museum." I was starting to relax with Wendy. She gave me a shy little smile.

"Hi, Hugo!" I waved.

He turned back to the milkshake dispenser, saying "Wuurrgghh!" and waving his arms about.

"Er, bye then mate," I said.

I sat down with my burger and fries, feeling a bit glum that Hugo didn't seem to remember me. The truth is, I was glad that Hugo was doing well. So what if I hardly saw him anymore? He had a job, he was doing well. I was happy for my friend.

Then I took a French fry from the packet.

Only, it wasn't.

It was a finger.

MEMORY OF WATER

George stirred the milk in his tea, making it just the right shade of brown. As he sipped, he glanced towards the escalators. Daniel was late. Just a matter of a few minutes, but George regarded punctuality as important, and it was disappointing that his son failed to recognise this. He could have allowed him that indulgence, just today. Just this once, do as he was asked at the time that he was asked to do it. He was the same as this when he was a boy: rarely defiantly disobedient, but often slow to follow through. Everything in his own time.

When Daniel did arrive, he was flustered, glancing at his watch as he took the seat opposite his father. His hair had grown since George had last seen him; it hung lank over his open collar. Still, at least the moustache had gone. Wispy and thin, it hadn't really worked.

"Hi Dad. Coffee?" he said, pointing at George's full cup.

"No. Tea."

"No, I mean do you want one?"

"This is fine. I like tea."

"Okay if I get one? I haven't got long and I need my mid-morning booster." He got up and made for the queue without waiting for an answer. Rules of manners have certainly changed, thought George. It used to be courtesy to seek permission of your company, now the courtesy seems to be just to *ask* the question. The answer was irrelevant. George used to insist that his children seek permission before leaving the table, no matter where they were. When did that stop? When did the father stop fathering the child? Still, at least he was here now.

Ten minutes later, Daniel was sitting opposite his father, setting his steaming cappuccino on the plastic table between them.

"Good to see you, Dad," he said, as he sipped froth.

"And you. How is work?"

"Well, busy, as ever. I have to get back soon. I have a meeting with the art department. Problems with the proofs – ah, you don't want to know about that. How are you, anyway?"

"Well, my neck has been playing up, and I get cold down one side of my leg if I walk too far or have to sit too long *waiting*. But those are my *old* ailments. But you haven't been too interested in that, have you? I wanted to..." said George, rubbing the side of his neck as he spoke.

Daniel tried not to roll his eyes. No matter how long it had been since his last conversation with his father, any discussion would always end up being about his aches and pains. Any cold that his father suffered was worse than anybody else's, and to suggest otherwise was considered disloyal or impudent. He felt nine years old again, and bristled. Fighting the instinct to get up and walk away, Daniel sipped his coffee and said nothing as his father trailed off.

"The shops look busy. Not surprising really, this close to Christmas," said Daniel, glancing over the escalators at the chain of stores and boutiques that snaked away across the concourse of bustling people.

George followed his gaze. Dozens of people, milling about, some rushing, some taking their time enjoying the shopping experience. Life goes on, and each of those people have their own lives, their own worlds, and so rarely will those worlds meet. He imagined each person as a living Venn diagram, each circle of experience intersecting that of only one or two other's in the whole place. What would they share, in that moment where their lives cross over? Irritation? Aggression? Humour? Intimacy? The life of his own son was itself a perfect circle that rarely even bounced off his. They had become familiar strangers.

"It's good to see you, Dad," Daniel said, deliberately seeking his father's eyes. He was looking for a hint of something that would tell him how to begin. George looked down at his tea, watching his hand stir the spoon in perfect circles as if it were someone else's. Both of them were on the verge of speaking, yet neither knew how to begin. Daniel sipped his coffee, thinking of the times when his father was absent, the childhood times when he needed him and pined for his return.

It was not Danny's day. It was one of those embarrassing times of having to go visiting, working down the checklist of interminable relatives, when Danny was crowbarred into politeness by his mother. He was having to peep out of his cocoon of private games and adventures of interplanetary war and Wild West gunfights, and play with a cousin he would rather have ignored. To the eleven-year-old Daniel King, his cousin Jeremy might as well have been a girl because he whined and cried whenever he didn't get his own way. He was two years older than Danny, but Danny had to be the biggest, bravest, most invulnerable ten year old ever in the history of the world. Mum needed him that way. He knew that.

Danny sat under the tree in the back garden amongst the wet autumn leaves, arms folded. His bottom lip protruded as far out as he could push it without it being too obvious that he was faking a snivel. He felt the dew from the wet morning grass and the brown, dying leaves gradually soak into the material of his underpants. The dew had already made its mark on the seat of his jeans. It was wet and it was cold. Still, if his plan was working, his mother would be watching and he was too far down the road on this particular sulk to give up now, no matter how sopping cold his backside was becoming. He huffed and tightened the fold of his arms. The tree above seemed to him to sigh in sympathy as a light morning breeze briefly swept through its upper branches, its breath freeing another leaf from its perch. The lone leaf, borne briefly aloft on a gentle current, was like an old, tired butterfly about to give up its life of flight, until it was swept over the high garden wall and away.

Another, altogether different, sigh escaped the lips of Danny's mother. Weary, Maggie King leaned against the refrigerator in her sister's kitchen and watched her son pouting in the damp grass of the back lawn. Absorbed in her son, she allowed her thoughts to drift towards the boy's father. She could almost visualise him in the same position: head in hands, fingers running through dark, heavy hair. It was strangely comforting to imagine. Seeing him in Danny, believing that he was still with them was dangerously easy.

"What if I tear Jerry away from that cartoon and send them both up the shop? We need some more veg for dinner anyway. Mags?"

Her sister's voice pulled her back abruptly. She rubbed her forehead with her fingertips as if trying to retune her brain. "I'm sorry, Helen," she said, still out-of-tune. "I don't know what to do with him half the time. It's no good shouting at him – he just digs in those heels. Just like his father. Always has been."

Helen Lewis smiled at the idea. "He really does miss him, doesn't he? Is he still... having nightmares?" The question was cautiously asked. She almost felt that she was breaching a taboo, but George, Maggie and Helen had grown up in the same street and, despite all that had happened, she still thought of him as the grubby boy with scabby knees who fixed her bicycle's puncture when she was five years old. He taught her to ride along without once putting her feet on the ground. Looking at the troubled ten-year old sulking in the back garden, all that she could see was George King at the same age. Yes, just like his father.

"Yes," replied Maggie. Quietly.

When Danny had first arrived at his Aunt Helen's house in Southampton, he did try to incite some stirring within the pallid and immobile flesh of his cousin, who treated television-watching as a religious obligation. Of course, this was more or less upon arrival, with a strict mother-order to "Try Harder This Time" still fresh in his mind. The threat of withdrawn chocolate privileges had no small effect on his decision to indeed 'try harder', but it seemed a vain effort. Danny had wanted to go out and play War. The nearby estate, with its maze of cul-de-sacs and sites of unfinished new houses, seemed a fantasy soldier's paradise. The building sites could have easily served as nuclear wastelands and the dark spaces behind garages as vantage spots for snipers. Danny tried to extol the obvious virtues of these playgrounds as the thresholds of more exciting worlds, but Jeremy preferred to flop down in front of the TV and watch one of those pathetic cartoons featuring poorly animated pink cats or something equally below Danny's contempt. He took one look at his cousin, as lacking in enthusiasm as a ripe tomato, and the stupid TV woman with a green rabbit glove puppet on her hand, and decided this was certainly not for him. That had been over an hour ago and Jeremy was still watching something. Probably the test card. Danny's underpants, meanwhile, were becoming wetter and colder as the morning wore on. Still, he was determined. He was not going to move. No way.

"Danny! Auntie Helen needs some vegetables and stuff from the shop! Want to go?" called his mother, now standing some yards away at the back door of the house.

Danny briefly considered his options. He could have ignored his mother. That would certainly get him the attention for which he had been sulking so hard, sitting in the wet. Unfortunately, it could also have the opposite effect. He would be similarly ignored, and he would have to stay wet. Forever. He knew his mother's tactics pretty well by now. Alternatively, he could have shouted back, "No! I want to go home!" which is what his heart was urging his lips to push out. That would have been unwise, though, because it would make it look like he disliked his Auntie Helen. Despite having a moronic dollop for a son, Auntie Helen was nice really. So, contrary to expectations, Danny stood up, patted his sopping wet bottom, and walked gingerly towards the house.

"Coming, Mum!" he called brightly.

Maggie eyed Danny suspiciously, remembering all the other times he had pretended to be interested in going to the shop just so that he could con her into letting him buy some sweets with the change.

Danny approached the door, one hand holding the heavy seat of his jeans away from his cheeks. Clearly, the thought of sweets had already entered his head, as his mouth was turning up at the corners at the sight of the five-pound note in his aunt's hand. Helen whispered something to his mother that he could not quite hear. Bending down so that their eyes met, she slid the money into the breast pocket of his shirt. Helen's freckled face was stern, but Danny could see her eyes betraying a perplexingly wicked smile.

"Oh thank you, Danny," she said. "You can take Jeremy with you if you want. Won't that be nice?"

Danny's face crumpled, looking as if he had just been told to pop a live, stinging wasp into his mouth. Sighing, Danny's aunt handed him a shopping list written on the back of an old envelope. The smile in her eye had suddenly lost is sheen. Danny's eyes ran over the list carefully. His reading age had always been well above his physical age, so he really had no problem decoding his aunt's lazy adult scrawl, which listed quantities of bread, potatoes, carrots and milk. He read it over and over, but nothing could change the fact that nowhere on the old brown envelope were the words 'sweets', 'chocolate' or even 'crisps'! Danny was puzzled. Where was his incentive to go? Had his mother forgotten to tell his aunt what the rules were? His eyes darted desperately from mother to aunt and back again. Both women stood above him, arms folded, wielding kettle and saucepan respectively.

"Mum…" he began.

"No sweets," she confirmed. How had she guessed? "Maybe if you'd come in when we asked you the first time, instead of being silly. But not now. Go to the shop and we'll see about getting something from the ice-cream man when he comes round later on. If you make a bit more effort with your cousin when you come back. Straight there and straight back, okay?"

"Okay," he sighed, resigned to his sweetless fate.

Suddenly exuberant, Danny tore down the street. He was pleased to leave behind his cry-baby cousin, and he was not ashamed to show it. Running along the pavement, kicking loose gravel as he went, Danny imagined his cousin back in the house, sitting in a corner by the TV, practising his next little whine. Retreating into his warm, contented shell of playing alone, Danny was slipping into his favourite games. Like a movie director, he always gave them exotic and exciting settings, but they only ever really existed in one location: in a place where he felt in control, where he belonged, where he could imagine his father may steam around the corner at any moment and berate him for playing out past his curfew. The time he spent in this world, despite the hazard of high adventure, was safe. It was his. It was free. It was the lofty enterprise and it was the great escape.

Danny was in turns the masked saviour of a crime-ridden city awash with pantomime villains; the gun-totin', rootin' tootin' cowboy heading for a showdown with the cigar-chomper in the black hat; and the sole survivor of an alien takeover of the planet, fighting on against robot duplicates of his family and friends. Today, he ran around the estate, ducking in and out of alleyways. He rolled away from the tentacles of invisible extra-terrestrials amid the sand of a building site empty for the weekend. He shot laser beams from his fingers and fashioned highly destructive bombs from fresh air, which he tossed into the gaping maw of a lumbering leviathan. Happy and brave and free and alone, he lost track of time and place.

Suddenly, the sun was not quite so bright or as high in the sky as it was. It was barely beyond mid-afternoon, but to Danny it could have been midnight. He looked around him and identikit new homes snaked and swirled and crowded and pushed into the distance in every direction. The newness, the unfamiliarity, the endlessness of it all seemed to shout and stare at him from the very brickwork. The game of being the solitary hero battling alone against a hostile world was suddenly too close to reality and not quite so exciting.

His imaginary laser pistol dissolved from his hand. His heart sank. Lost and afraid in an empty and silent street, Danny sat down by the roadside and started to cry. The neighbours who stared at him disapprovingly through twitching curtains in cloned houses suddenly seemed more threatening to him than even the android army of the alien invaders.

A rotund, ruddy middle-aged woman emerged from the nearest house, half concerned and half irritated by the child's wailing. Danny drew in a sharp breath of surprise as she knelt down beside him, floral print dress barely covering her pink and bulbous knees. She fingered the plastic curlers in her brown-and-grey hair and rested the thick digits of her other hand on Danny's shoulder.

"Are you all right?" she said. "Have you lost your Mummy?"

Danny, sore-eyed and trembling, was too scared to answer.

"You can come in and sit down if you want. It's cold out here, isn't it?" she continued evenly. She sounded kind and patient but it seemed like an effort.

Danny looked up at her through hot, red eyes. She was a stranger, as unknown to him and as sinister as any dark, helmeted enemy of the crime-ridden metropolis of his games. His lips too numb with fear to allow him to speak, he pulled, involuntarily. His fear ruled him totally. He ran and ran and ran until fire burned through every avenue in his chest. Tears once again cracked the steel façade of the hardened hero of adventure. He no longer felt much like a hero. When it came down to it, the aliens' planet of burning rock was a much more friendly place than the streets near his cousin's house.

Far behind him now, the curlered woman groaned herself to her feet and shuffled back to her house, the plight of a lost child forgotten as a glance at her plastic wristwatch reminded her that it was time for her daily dose of *Pebble Mill At One*: television anaesthesia at its most potent.

Danny ran and ran until he was too far away even to find where he had become lost before. Trees lined this street. The houses were older – tall and Victorian. The pavement was leafy and brown and welcoming. It seemed to wrap him in its arms, offering warmth and rest. He leaned against one of the thickest of the trees and clung tightly to the hard, sturdy support and solid protection of the bark, as if trying to become part of the tree. The tears and chokes and sobs came again. For some minutes, he cried out for Mum and Dad. Mostly Dad. Still he was alone, his eyes squeezed tight against the world.

The warm, purring sound of an approaching engine caught his breath. As he lifted his head and opened his eyes, the sound grew closer and louder, the gentle turn of the engine as soothing and comfortable as home. On schooldays, before his father went away, Danny would sit in front of *Blue Peter* (not really enjoying it) keeping one ear on the television and one on the drive, waiting for the car to pull up, carrying Dad home from work. With Dad at home, everything could be smooth and even.

Danny saw the door catch being released and the door slowly swing open at the kerb, mere inches away. Tears of relief began to sear his cheeks, already sore from where the tears of fear had been. Excited, he was oblivious to all but the opening door.

He grabbed the handle. Started to climb in. All was a haze, a fog, a helter skelter of mixed sense and feeling. He had seen a car, a door, a seat, a driver, but not taken note of colour, shape of definition. His hand was pulling the door shut, ready to secure his safety back in the familiar surroundings of his father's car. He sat in the dry, soft passenger seat. Froze when he focused and saw that the beckoning, smiling face of the solitary driver did not belong to his father. Or his mother. Or his aunt.

He ran.

The man in the car had been smiling but it was a smile that had frightened Danny. He thought of the gunfighter in the black hat. In Danny's games, the gunfighter had had a smile like that: full of tobacco and dirty stubble. The difference was that the driver had not been wearing a black hat or gun belt. Instead, he had a car and a smile and a face of intent that Danny did not like. Beyond the cacophony of blood pounding in his ears, Danny heard the screech of tyres and the engine burst into a harsher roar as the stranger and his car disappeared into the distance behind, the roar growing weaker as Danny ran further.

As Maggie looked out at the darkening sky, she trembled involuntarily. A thousand scenarios cascaded through her head. Mentally shaking herself, she dismissed each possibility one by one. Danny was going to come home soon. Danny was going to be safe. Outside, clouds seemed to huddle and conspire together, growing darker with each raindrop tapping at the window or stabbing at the ground. Each one was a needle sewing tighter the band of fear around her chest. Hours had passed since Danny left the house, note clutched in his creamy fist, trainers thudding against paving.

"Still no sign?" asked her sister.

Maggie turned from the window and, shaking her head, accepted the offered mug of tea.

"Careful, the sides are hot. It's the china one. Doesn't hold the heat very well," said Helen, holding her own mug now in trembling hands. The paleness of Maggie's face told her everything she was beginning to feel herself.

"He can't be just lost. Something must've… Oh, Helen, he misses his Dad so much…" Maggie's voice lost itself in swallowing a sob, tears welling in her tired eyes.

Helen placed her tea down on the nearby table and held an arm around her sister's shoulders, pressing her forehead against Maggie's, as if trying to stave off the tears of both women. For a time, they froze in the moment until Maggie broke the silence.

"I'm going to phone the police," she said. She moved into the hall and picked up the receiver. Helen followed her.

Her unspoken question hung in the air as Maggie dialled the number.

Outside, the rain, like silver splinters, grew more persistent against the window. Inside, huddled beside a cold and unforgiving radiator, Danny listened. Tap tap tap. Danny was wearing only the jeans, shirt and well-worn trainers that he had left his aunt's house with hours earlier. Scant protection from the hardness of the floor and the cold of the early evening. The loose window catch rattled. Danny had found it open, offering him his only refuge from the rain. It now resisted all attempts to close it, as if eager to beckon in any and all seeking shelter. That prospect was not one that appealed to him at all.

Enough twilight was getting through the thickening rain and the dusty window to outline the dimensions of the room; enough to confirm what the rugby posts in the field outside had already suggested to Danny. Losing his way across the fields at the rear of the housing estate, which he thought led to his aunt's road, he had found himself in the grounds of a school. Not his own. He knew that, but the central features were pretty much universal. Tables with veneered tops, absently carved and scribbled upon in various places, shared floor space with legs bent the wrong way or otherwise mangled by forces which nature only endows children with when they are in a classroom. An array of open, bent lockers stood against the rear wall. Dog-eared or torn sheets of sugar paper, which once held examples of pupils' felt-tipped 'best' work, hung wearily from defiant staples on display boards around the room. The blackboard's faint powdery smear betrayed the inexplicable interaction of numbers and letters: inexplicable to Danny, at least. Daniel King. Ten years old and shuddering.

A classroom. A daytime thing. Not a place for moonlight and shadows, but for chalk and chatter. The silence, broken only by the intermittent straining of the window catch and the irregular ticking of the rain, pressed in on him like a blanket, although lacking its warmth and comfort. The radiator felt as if it had never known heat but still Danny embraced it with damp and trembling arms.

Tap tap tap. The rain.

Tap.

Not the rain now. Duller.

Tap taptap. Closer.

Tap. A pause. Footsteps!

A thousand imagined nemeses rushed to Danny's chest as it tightened in fear. The aliens! The enemy soldiers! The gunfighter! The man in the car! A door creaked. Danny's eyes shot towards the sound. From the corridor, a beam of torchlight cut through the gap between door and frame, pulling in a hunched figure with it.

The face of the figure smiled dimly from within the shadows. His heart pumping too much to allow him to speak, Danny sucked in breath after breath, trying desperately to call for help.

The darkness was pushed away as light flicked into every corner of the room at once. Danny blinked at the sudden glare of the fluorescent tubes above his head. Standing against the wall, finger still resting on the light switch, the figure regarded the child with faint amusement. After the spots had cleared from Danny's frantically blinking eyes, he looked up at the old man standing opposite, nonchalantly smirking and stroking his dry, grey beard with the rubber end of his torch.

"Good evening, lad," said the man, a hint of a just-buried Irish accent lingering on the vowels of his soft drawl.

Danny's lips fell loosely open, as inarticulate as rubber. The man's face was creased and cracked like old paving and his hair thinned from white tufts above the ears to shining absence atop his head. Wrinkles darted in all directions as he grinned and winked; yet the skin around his eyes seemed to be so soft that it glowed. Absorbed in this new wonder, Danny almost forgot his fear, although the voice deep in his head was whispering *"Don't talk to strangers!"* over and over.

"Breakin' and enterin' is a serious charge, y'know, lad," toyed the old man.

That did the trick.

Indignant at the accusation, the boy pulled himself to his feet, clutching the radiator both as a support and, desperately, as a comfort. "I didn't!" he protested. "I got lost and it was raining and the window was already open and it was cold! It was c..."

He broke off as his throat dried and tears filled his eyes.

"Hush, lad," said the old man, taking one step forward, a hand extended, palm up as a gesture of trust. "Y' got nothin' to fear from me. Been caretaker of this place for nigh on... well, too many year than I care to remember, believe me. Come on, we'll get ye a nice cup o' tea and then maybe we'll..."

"I want to go home. I got lost," Danny mumbled.

"Aye, son. Soon as ye like. In the meantime, let's get ye warmed up."

Sliding his torch neatly into a conveniently-sized pocket in his blue overalls, the caretaker placed a warm, veined hand on the boy's shivering shoulder and led him gently out into the corridor. Clicking wall switches as they went, Danny's gentle companion revealed a route through corridors of peeling paint and decade-old murals, with photographs of school sports teams and posters for long-closed sixth form drama productions arranged haphazardly at strategic points near doorways and staircases along the way. Finally, they came to a small room, really little more than a converted cupboard, marked 'Caretaker's Office'. The musty school smell gave way to a mustier cupboard smell as the old man opened the door and ushered Danny in.

The room had indeed been used as a store cupboard once, the man explained, but it served well as a place to pause and drink tea or sneak a few minutes' repose once in a while. Danny sat in a careworn old armchair rescued from a staff room clear-out, whilst an upturned plastic crate served the caretaker just as well as he sat and lit his strictly forbidden camping stove and placed his already half-full kettle over the flame to boil. Aside from a pile of damp cardboard boxes heaped up behind the armchair, there was little room and certainly little need for much else in the old man's cramped sanctum.

Watching the kettle intently, the man asked, without looking up, "Won't your mam be worrying about you by now?"

"Yes," sighed Danny, not really taking in the question. He was relaxing, sinking into the dusty warmth of the chair. "She only sent me to the shop and I was playing and… We don't live round here."

There was something in the old man's embracing smile that disarmed his natural child's fear, but Danny felt as if he had already said too much.

Taking an enamelled metal cup from a small cardboard box on the floor, the man said, "No. I could tell. Me neither. Not anymore, anyway."

He handed Danny the cup. Taking it, Danny noticed the name 'Ruskin' scratched into the enamel on one side. Seeing the boy mouth the unfamiliar new word to himself, the wrinkled stranger rubbed the bush on his chin with his thumb and said, "Aye. Ruskin. Ruskin Claverty. That's my name." He chuckled. "Ye can blame me parents."

Ruskin Claverty pointed at the mug cradled in Danny's hands. "I've 'ad that mug since I was in the army. Been with me through thick and thin. Tea tastes lifeless out of any other mug. Magic tea in that mug."

Danny giggled. "That's stupid. No such thing. My dad says…" He stopped, mid-sentence, and cast his eyes down into the empty mug. His bottom lip began to quiver.

As if he had not noticed, Claverty picked up the thread, adding, "I tried a flask once. Not hot enough. Not magic at all." He paused, but the boy's eyes remained cast downwards. "Aye," he continued, "Dads always know, don't they? I remember, my old Da, he..."

"*I* don't." Danny sounded sullen.

"Eh?"

"My dad. I don't remember him, sometimes. I have to think hard to remember what he looks like. Sometimes."

Claverty leaned forward and placed the tip of his finger on Danny's knee, causing him to look up and their eyes to meet. His gaze seemed to Danny to aim at something past his eyes, something deep inside his head. The old man's brow furrowed and the soft lilt of his voice became firmer, more solid, hinting at another accent that Danny could not name. "Never forget, lad. He remembers you and, as long as you miss him, he will be right here," he said, tapping Danny's temple with the tip of the same finger.

His eyes fixed on the man's hand as he rested it now on his own knee, Danny said, "He's not *dead*. Just gone away with work. He always comes back eventually, but this time it's been ages."

The sound of the kettle whistling interrupted them. Claverty rummaged in his box on the floor, took out teabags, powdered milk and a half-bag of sugar, then set to work on the tea. As he busied himself methodically and quietly, Danny swung his legs back and forth, dangling over the edge of the chair. He felt comfortable. Tea was made, which he sipped carefully from the enamel mug. Claverty drank from a cracked china mug, which was his spare. Danny felt honoured that he had been allowed to drink from a mug with such an heroic history.

"Sometimes I wish he wouldn't come back," he said, almost matter-of-factly. The words were out, finally given voice, before he realised the full weight of them.

Ruskin Claverty sipped his tea thoughtfully, then placed his mug down on the floor, wiping the residue from his moustache with the back of his hand. He leaned in close to Danny, his withered smile washing a warm wave over the boy.

"No, Danny," the old man said simply. "We would not be having this chat if ye did. And remember: nothing in your life is bad enough to hide away from. Not even family."

Danny yawned, the evening weighing him down. It did not occur to him until later that he had not mentioned his name to the old man. Yet he knew. His eyelids began to flutter.

"Little t'be afraid of in sleep neither, lad. There's secrets and there's truths in sleep. Remember that one and ye won't go far wrong."

Bathed in a buoyant feeling of trust, Danny settled back into the chair and allowed his eyes to close, his lids at first fluttering like tired butterflies. With his new friend nearby, he was unexpectedly safe and secure. And brave. And free.

Danny rubbed his eyes vigorously.

"Dad?" he whispered.

No. Not here. He looked around him, blinking through tears, at the storeroom. Musty and cramped, as it he remembered it. An enamel mug sat on the floor, empty.

He climbed down from the chair and stepped into the corridor. His heart pushed at his chest, as if trying to escape; beating, beating. He looked up and down, hazy sunlight spray-painting the dust in the air at the far end. No Ruskin Claverty. No kindly old man. Only the mug and the memory.

The police van came across Danny at around six a.m. He was squeezing through the bars of the locked main gate of Green Vale Secondary Modern at the time. Nervously, he climbed into the back of the police car, bleary-eyed but otherwise unperturbed. Danny absently watched the streets and trees whip by as the policewoman in the front passenger seat called in the news of his safe recovery to another officer on the car's radio. She had introduced herself as 'WPC Annie McNeil', which he thought sounded like one of *Charlie's Angels*. Finished, she placed the handset back in its cradle and turned to look at Danny. She rested her cheek against the side of the headrest. She was blonde and she was nice, Danny noted as she drew his attention away from the blurs passing by the window.

"There you are, Daniel. Your mummy's being told now that you're coming home. Are you all right?" she said in her cheery, children's TV presenter-pitch voice.

Danny nodded.

"Mm. Good."

"How did you get into the school, mate?" chimed in the driver, a PC Dave Cordon, who had shaken Danny's hand so firmly on introducing himself that it had hurt the bones in his fingers. Man to man, that was. He liked that.

"Window," he replied.

"Better get that looked at," said Cordon to his partner. "That block of the school has been closed up for a year. They haven't used it since they built the new science block. They're supposed to knock it down soon and put up a new building in its place. The Head's a stickler for security, so he won't be too chuffed, hearing from us again."

"Mm," agreed Annie. "Are you hungry? Thirsty?"

"Could do with a coffee, I've got …"

"Not you, you twit. I was talking to Danny here." She smiled at the boy, rolling her eyes in the direction of the driver. "I think Dave's got a flask here somewhere."

"Oi!" Cordon protested.

"No. I'm okay thank you," said Danny quietly.

"Did you say you made a cup of tea last night, Danny?" she asked, her brow knotting above her nose.

"No. Ruskin did. Mister Claverty. The caretaker man."

The car had paused at traffic lights. The two police officers exchanged confused glances at Danny's mention of Claverty. Annie opened her mouth to say something else, but a squeeze on the arm from her colleague stopped her. The remainder of the journey contained the usual adult-to-child conversation concerning favourite football teams, favourite subjects at school, the two adults hedging around the topic of the previous night.

Almost before the doorbell rang, Maggie's hands were scrambling for the front door. She fell on her son immediately,

172

arms enfolding him, sobs damping his head. No recriminations, no apologies. Explanations could come later.

Sucking on an ice-lolly beside his mother on the sofa in his aunt's sitting room, Danny told his story, even recounting snatches of his chat with the old caretaker. He shared jokes with his cousin, who suddenly seemed much less childish. What had happened to change Jeremy overnight? he wondered. His aunt served tea to the police officers as they sat and listened in the sitting room, the bright morning sun streaming in through the window.

Satisfied that no harm had been done to the boy or to any property, the police took their leave to go. Maggie thanked them and ushered Danny up the stairs into the bathroom for a hot bath, accompanied by the normal protestations of "Aw, Mum!" though even Danny knew that, where bath time was concerned, mothers ruled. So he grudgingly went along with it.

As mother and son scrubbed and splashed upstairs, Helen stood on the doorstep with Annie MacNeil. Dave Cordon waited impatiently in the car, tapping his watch.

"Well, thanks again. We were so worried, what with the way he's been acting lately. His father is… hasn't been around for a while and he's at that age where they start to ask different kinds of questions, so, y'know…"

"Mmm. Kids have vivid imaginations that come to the fore when they don't get the answers that they're looking for sometimes." Cordon sounded the horn. She mouthed 'wait' at him.

"Good thing that caretaker was there to keep him out of the rain. Will he still be at the school, do you know? Or does he just work nights? I think Maggie would like to thank him."

The policewoman glanced back at the car. She fiddled uncomfortably with her hat that she held in her hands, her thumb tracing the rim. She paused, then said, "That would be a bit difficult."

"Why?"

"Well, you see, I went to Green Vale myself, as did Dave. Small world, eh? Anyway, I left... mm... *years* ago. God, makes me feel old, thinking of it like that. My little sister is still there, in the Sixth Form. Mister Claverty was the caretaker until about a year ago. He was a right old character – he was Irish but he'd been all over the world, so he had a story for every occasion. We used to make fun of that, but he liked us kids. He – um – liked *some* of the girls a bit too much, if you know what I mean. There was a bit of gossip about that at one point, but I don't know if anything ever came of it. Probably just malicious rumour. The thing is, I don't know where Danny heard about

174

him from, but he *couldn't* have been with him last night. He just isn't there anymore. One morning, apparently, one of the cleaners found him slumped in an old armchair in his little storeroom, old enamel cup still in his hand. It seems he died in his sleep. Or he deliberately drank himself to death, depending on which story you believe. And that was over a year ago."

As Helen waved the car off, she decided not to mention her doorstep conversation with the policewoman to her sister. In time, both Maggie and Danny forgot about Claverty the caretaker. At least, neither mentioned him to Helen again. Still, for Danny, the memory of that night itched below the surface of his thoughts for years to come, never fully realised but always with him, like a half-aware haunting. In dark nights, when the rain would lash against the window, he would cry out for his father in his sleep, only to forget when he awoke. And his aunt never forgot the shiver she felt as she stood on the step that autumn morning.

Danny was eleven, going on twelve. He was proud of that, kind of: just one step closer to closer to the magical teenage years that were supposed to be so full of fun and freedom. And girls. He had begun to notice this important feature of secondary school life, although only two months into his first term of the first year. He would sit in maths class and stare, eyes glazed, at Linda Butcher, twelve years old, slender and fond of tossing her long, shiny black hair this way over that shoulder, that way over this shoulder, whenever anyone was looking. Danny liked the way the sunshine flashed off it when she did that. He even tried to speak to her once as they waited outside the maths room, but she brushed past before he could extinguish his burning cheeks and deflate his swollen lips, which always seemed to suddenly impair his ability to articulate sensible words in such situations. It was the same when he tried to ask Hannah Bennett the time, and he didn't even fancy her.

It was a nightmare that he lived every day. The smell of a female classmate's cheap perfume, the sight of older girls in their seemingly ever-tighter skirts, and even the swell of certain teachers when they leaned forward or reached to the top of the blackboard: all these things excited Danny in ways of which he hitherto had no understanding. In fact, Danny was turning into a giant, throbbing tower of testosterone. Puberty had pounced on him like revenge. It was like a malfunctioning car alarm. It seemed that a mere gust of perfume would be enough to set it off. Sometimes, Danny would lie awake at night, stifling his sobs in a tear-soaked pillow, crying in whispers for his father to make it go away. He couldn't talk to his mother about it – mothers don't talk to their sons about things like that. Fathers do.

At school, Danny often sat alone. At break time, he usually stood alone in the playground, sometimes leaning against a wall with a comic, sometimes with nothing. Talking to others was a torment. His peers were so much more confident than him, so much more interesting to each other. So much unlike him.

On one cold November morning, Danny sat on a bench on the far side of the playground, his shoes scuffing back and forth on the tarmac as he swung them absently. Brown and red leaves twisted in the air, scooped up by Danny's kicks, only to fall again, settling gently on the soggy pile collecting beneath the bench. He stopped and turned his attentions to his rucksack. He was rooting for a packet of crisps when a mud-streaked plastic football arced up in the air and landed a few inches away from his feet.

"Oi! Pus'ead!" shouted a voice.

Unhearing, Danny began pulling out his rugby kit, searching for his snack.

"E's bloody ignorin' me!" exclaimed an indignant Tommy Fuller, the broad, burly, crew-cutted fourteen-year old scourge of the playground.

Tommy had been kicking a ball, which he had procured earlier from a skinny first year, against the wall of the sports hall, along with his would-be fellow bully, Dean Willis. Dean was thinner and smaller than Tommy, but he sported a similar haircut and similar bravado when coming across anyone quiet and unassuming. The object of the game had been to rebound the ball off the wall into the other player's testicles. Not surprisingly, only Tommy had succeeded in scoring any points thus far.

"Leave it, Tommy. It's a crap ball anyway. Bell's about to go," reasoned Dean, desperate to let his aching body parts recover.

Ignoring Dean's words, Tommy dragged his friend by the sleeve of his blazer, pushing some smaller children out of the way, to where Danny was sitting, rummaging in his bag. The yellow-and-brown ball idled at his feet.

"Oi! Why didn't you kick my ball back, pus'ead?" Tommy taunted. He kicked Danny's shin with the toe of his heavy non-school uniform trainers.

Leg smarting, Danny looked up sharply at the elder boy. His eyes wide and wet, he flushed red.

"Wuh-what?" he stammered.

"Pus. Head. You've got a head of pus. Pus'ead."

"No, I mean what ball?"

Dean, a physical extension of Tommy's will, picked up the football and flicked it at Danny's face. Being light and plastic, it bounced easily off and away down the playground. It stung. It stung like the time his mother slapped him for knocking a vase over in a temper. That vase had been a wedding present. Instantly, his face exploded into tears and wails. He flew at Dean Willis with fists and kicks of his own.

When a teacher finally arrived to prise the two boys apart, a ring of male and female pupils, like passers-by at a road accident, had formed around them. They chanted, "Scrap! Scrap!" as Dean's nose gushed blood onto Danny's knuckles.

Later that day, Danny sat with his mother in the office of the school's Deputy Head, a Mr Pontefract. Pontefract was a dispassionate man, deliberately detached from the concerns of the children and staff in his charge. Curiously, he always carried a calculator in the breast pocket of his tweed jacket, often taking it out in the middle of delivering a lesson in order to tap

179

in some secret number. The significance of this remained a mystery to all but Pontefract, but Danny liked to entertain the fantasy that the calculator was in fact a cleverly disguised code transmitter. Quite where or why the balding, stout man was transmitting his data were endlessly fascinating questions. In one scenario, the man had been replaced with an exact copy by aliens and had successfully infiltrated the education system in order to brainwash the nation's youth with the propaganda of his planet's leader, the evil and insidious Count Pythagoras. In reality, the fifty-two year old Geoffrey Pontefract lived with his mother near the bingo hall and his sole interest was his work. Numbers. The interplay and arrangement of them held an almost hypnotic interest for him; so much so that he kept his pocket calculator in his pocket at all times.

Danny watched Pontefract's index finger tap rhythmically on the equals button of the calculator on the desk in front of him. The display flashed in time with each tap as the numerical total changed. Danny wondered how long he could go on before his finger succumbed to an arthritic seizure or the batteries ran out.

"You see, Mrs King," he said, eyes half on the screen, "Young Daniel here has broken a school rule and we have very clearly defined penalties for those who break the rules."

Tap tap.

Noticing the object of Danny's concentration, Maggie nudged her son gently. He blinked to attention.

"I don't think you understand what Danny has been through over the past couple of years. We…his father and I… we split up."

"Yes, Mrs King. I sympathise, but from what the other boys have told us, Danny's outburst was over a football, not anything else. He knows that fighting is strictly forbidden in school, and of course it's not the first time that his temper has gotten the better of him."

Tap.

"We haven't been here for more than a few months – we moved here to be near my mother - and Danny finds it hard to fit in. I don't think being bullied helps him to do that," she bristled. "Now, what are *you* doing to do about the boys who picked on him?"

The air was sparking. A confrontation was building, like a thunderstorm.

Pontefract stopped tapping. He leaned over the desk, fingers pressing down on the cheap veneer.

"Well," he said, "Daniel does not seem to have tried his utmost to make friends. He isolates himself from his classmates and today reacted violently when some older boys asked him to return their ball. Perhaps it would do Daniel more good to take two days to think about how he might try to fit into school life a little more…"

Danny stared at the teacher's nicotine-stained fingertips, turning white as they pressed down on the tabletop.

"Are you *suspending* my son?"

The shrillness in his mother's voice made him jump.

"Rules are rules, Mrs…"

Margaret King stood quickly, wrenching Danny from his chair. Trembling, holding in her own anger and tears just barely, she pointed a finger at Pontefract. Her knuckles seemed to strain against the skin covering them, ready to leap out and rap his nose. "There's only one rule that I'm interested in. And that's to do with you providing my son with an education. He *will* be in school tomorrow or I'll hold you personally responsible for providing childcare for my son whilst I'm out earning money to feed and clothe him. Is that clear or do I have to translate it into binary code for you?"

He seemed stunned, like a bird that had just flown into a windscreen. A mother who knew what binary code was. As his mouth dropped open, she glanced down with disdain at his pocket calculator. Nervously, his hand hovered over it, his security blanket. She swept out of the room, clutching her son close to her side.

Danny and his mother walked home in silence. She held his hand tightly and he looked up into her dark, lost eyes with new admiration. His fingers closed around hers; squeezing so that he could feel his mother's knuckles in his hand.

"I wish Dad was here," he said quietly.

She squeezed his hand more tightly and took him home.

That evening, Danny slept fitfully. In the darkness, every time he closed his eyes, Tommy Fuller taunted and kicked and pushed him. He kept his hands tucked under the pillow, behind his head, clenched into fists, and thought about his father: about how his father would have shown him how to beat those bullies. About how much happier his mother would be, how she wouldn't have to fight all his battles for him if only…

If only.

Once in the night, Danny thought he heard his mother crying, but by then he was too tired and the heavy hands of sleep soon drew him down.

Danny and his mother lived in Tenby, a small holiday town on the Pembrokeshire coast. One day, during a hot Welsh summer, he came home with a friend.

Maggie worked late shifts at the seaside café where she had been serving teas and ice creams since the season began. She and Danny lived with her parents at the Cliff Rise Guest House, which they owned and ran – their retirement gift to each other. Danny regarded the place as an adventure. The maze of rooms and floors and cubby holes in the eighteenth-century building was a playground of all colours to him, and often he would startle guests by running up and down stairs and corridors, shooting at invisible enemies with his pointed fingers.

That day, as Maggie watched Danny run up the garden to the back door of the hotel, his new friend trailing behind, she thanked God that he had only just celebrated his twelfth birthday. Not grown up yet. She was peeling potatoes at the sink, taking care not to splash dirty water on the black skirt and white blouse that comprised her café uniform. Mary, her mother, Danny's no-nonsense Gran, prepared cutlery for the evening meal on the worktop behind her daughter. She was in her late fifties, but fit and leathery with it, rarely seen out of her trademark t-shirt and tracksuit bottoms. In her younger days, she and her husband had run a successful boating business for tourists, operating from a hut near the far end of Westby's South Beach. They would take families out along the coast and, later, her husband would take novice divers out into shallow waters to learn promptly-forgotten scuba skills. More experienced customers would be treated to an underwater swim over an old nineteenth century boat wreck two miles offshore. Those days were but pleasant memories now, especially as her husband Bill's heart had finally given in to too many years of nicotine and whisky. Her weakness was a cream tea and she tried to steer away from them as much as possible, although that had become more than a little difficult since her daughter began working in a shop that served scones mounded with clotted cream and sticky sweet jam every afternoon.

Danny burst through the door, surging through the narrow gap between the two women.

"Come on!" he called to his friend, who paused quietly, blushing, at the door.

"Wait just one minute!" shrilled his mother, trying to be stern. "Aren't you going to introduce us to your friend?"

Danny pulled the other boy into the kitchen by the sleeve.

"Sorry, Mum. This is Carl. I thought I'd show him my comics. He draws a brilliant Desperate Dan!"

With that, Carl waved a brief hello as Danny whisked him up the stairs to his room. Maggie listened to the thudding and laughing, growing duller as they climbed the flights past the guest rooms to Danny's on the top floor. Mother and grandmother exchanged smiles.

In the coming months, Carl's visits to the hotel would become more frequent. Always he would wear a ragged old anorak, even at the height of summer, and black-rimmed spectacles, sellotaped at the centre to hold together an old break. He was a skinny lad who smiled almost inanely, never seeming to the women to say anything other than 'hello', 'goodbye', 'please' and 'thank you'. Seen but not heard. Ideal in many respects, not least because he was someone with whom Danny seemed to connect. A smile spread across Maggie's face whenever she heard laughter or sounds of pretend gunfire filter down from upstairs. It always meant that Danny was happy. Gradually, Carl was followed by a small circle of boys, all playing happily outside or in Danny's room whenever they came around. After months of begging, Danny's grandparents bought him a video game system as a birthday present, and the boys swapped games and enthused over computer magazines for hours on end at the kitchen table. Everything seemed to be coming together. The café stayed open during the winter and Maggie was appointed manageress. Although business was poor in the quiet months, the café kept ticking over with weekend trade from the locals. Danny was certainly happier. Only occasionally would she now hear muffled sobs in Danny's sleep, but days went by each time without him mentioning anything, so she always let things alone. After all, every outward sign suggested that Danny was happier than he had ever been.

The winter came and went. Spring bounced along, and by the time of the Easter holiday, the town swelled with visitors once more. As had become their habit, Danny and his friends played football on the beach when the days were breezier.

It was indeed a breezy afternoon. Danny, Carl, Pete Osbourne and Darren Platts played two-against-two on the beach. Pete and Carl stood in the goals, each one marked out on the sand by stray seaweed and pebbles. Pete was round and puffy, his tee shirt rising up over his blancmange stomach each time that he lumbered towards the ball. The other boys sometimes deliberately tapped the ball wide, Pete's wobbling tyre giving them an easy laugh. He always smiled, though: never caught without a smart riposte. Each remark about his portly posture was parried with a swipe at Danny's spotty chin, Carl's still-sellotaped spectacles, or Darren's legendary flatulence. Carl, being lighter than Pete, conceded fewer goals.

As soon as Danny had scored his fifth against Pete, the ball was returned to the centre of their makeshift pitch and Darren took a new kick. The only 'real' footballer in the group, Darren played for the school and, with his toothy grin and blond curls, he even looked the part.

Danny tackled, his toe just stretching enough to flick the ball past Darren's reach. Both boys, feet tumbling through the thick sand, pursued the cheap plastic ball as it bounced away along the sand. A gust lifted it up, above and beyond their heads, towards the rocks at the shoreline. At this end of the South Beach, the sand thinned and curved around the base of a jutting cliff. A series of rocks bolstered the cliff's base, some of which were climbable, some only steppable. One or two slippery climbs led to entrances into black caves, many of which burrowed deep into the cliff. Most were to narrow to crawl through, but many made admirable hiding places. Even when the tide was out, waves would lick against the base of the rocks, making it impossible to reach the other side of the cliff even when the tide was out. Over the rocks lay the beginnings of the North Beach, just a few frustrating metres away. For Danny and his moderately intrepid friends, the rocks never made too difficult an obstacle but for the spray and seaweed making clambering over the boundary too slippery to be worth the effort. The ball bounced back off one of the lower rocks, just kissing the lip of the surf.

His lank black hair flapping against his eyes, Danny reached the ball first and scooped it up with his foot, booting it back to his goalkeeper. It was a high kick and Carl was in no way inclined to leap up and grab it. The ball arced high, landed, bounced with that loud, hollow twang that cheap balls make, then settled at the base of a set of concrete steps that led up to the promenade above. The ball began to roll back towards the make-do pitch.

Leaning on a rail at the top of the steps were Tommy Fuller and Dean Willis. Wrapping their tongues around sloppy ice-creams, they watched.

Although Danny and his friends went to the same school as the two would-be thugs, they were in different year groups, used different playgrounds (in theory anyway), and Tommy and Dean were notorious truants. Consequently, their paths rarely crossed since the previous year's playground encounter. Danny looked up in dread. All weight drained from his stomach. He felt as if he were on the moon.

"Oi!" Chuck us the ball!" commanded Tommy to Carl.

Carl stooped down to pick up the ball as gravity rolled it to his feet. Carl could not think of an answer that would not provoke the older boy, so he said nothing, cradling the ball under his arm.

Pete plodded over to join his friend. He turned to look up at the two bullies.

"Do they usually let you out without a lead?" he called out, with sudden bravado. "Be careful the dog catcher don't see ya!"

Carl pushed him in the chest, forcing the air out. Pete coughed, staggered back, and stumbled against a hillock of sand. "Pete! What are you trying to do? Get our heads kicked in?" Carl said, his voice rising to a squeal.

Either Tommy misheard or failed to understand, as he seemed not to react to the insult. All the same, he started walking down the steps. Carl had expected full pelt, fists flying, a mouth full of gritty sand. Dean was close behind his compatriot, his big, loose trainers slapping like wet fish on the concrete.

"Go on, give us a game. Me and Dean against the rest of ya, except we'll have Specky in goal," Tommy slurped through his melting ice cream.

Carl's grip on the ball tightened. "Don't call me Specky," he said, irritated.

Danny and Darren now stood behind Carl. Pete wheezed over to one side of him. Darren, good-looking and popular, spoke up. "All right, Tommy! Hiya Dean," he laughed. It was the same false laugh that his father used on meeting neighbours or work colleagues in the street. "We're just playing two-on-two. Besides, you two are bigger than us. We'd stand no chance, would we?"

Danny piped up. He imagined they each had their gun hands hovering over an invisible holster. "Anyway, you're eating ice creams," he ventured. "You can't play with them in your hands."

Noticing Danny for the first time, and recognising him straight away, Tommy dropped his fifty pence cone in the sand and snatched the ball from under Carl's arm. "Not any more!" he laughed, dropping the ball to his feet and dribbling it in the direction of the shore. Dean finished his cone, shoving the last splinters of wafer in his mouth. Flakes of cone sprayed between his lips as, giggling, he joined Tommy on the makeshift pitch. They punted the ball back and forth to each other, each time trapping the ball heavily with heels of their trainers.

"Come on then!" shouted Tommy.

"Wanker," Pete muttered under his recovered breath.

The four friends stood together, nervous. Darren adopted a big-brotherly, smooth-it-all-over tone. "If we have a quick kickabout with them, they'll go away again. It'll be all right," he said. Unconvincingly.

Danny glowered. A sense of injustice bubbled in his chest. Grinding his teeth, he imagined punching the bullies' faces. What was it with these two and footballs anyway?

In a temper, Carl stamped his foot, throwing sand up and into his shoe. "But he called me Specky!" he protested. "And he beat up Danny!"

"When?" asked Darren.

"Oh, ages ago. You were at football training when he told us. Well, I'm not playing. That twat called me Specky!"

"Well, we've got to do something," sighed Pete. "My Dad bought me that ball before he went to work in Saudi. I want it back."

Darren watched them pounding the ball with their feet. "It's only a crap one though. We can get another one."

Danny's eyes narrowed. He said firmly, "We'd better play them. As soon as we can, one of us grab the ball and then we'll run to my grandparents' place. It's not far."

"Well, I'm not grabbing it. They'll hit me," said Carl.

"Oh, shut up Specky," laughed Darren as they all trudged back to the pitch.

From Tommy and Dean's first few kicks of the ball, it was obvious that the younger boys' fears were not unfounded. The two older boys booted the ball back and forth between themselves, too hard for the others to easily intercept it. Darren attempted a tackle but was shoved out of the way by Dean, landing sprawling on the sand. Spitting gritty grains, Darren gathered himself. He ran between the two bullies, snatching the ball with his right foot then trapping it between his ankles. He spun and kicked it back along the beach to Pete. As Pete bent to pick it up, Tommy threw a handful of sand in his face. The coarse, sharp grains stung in his eyes and made him sneeze. The violence of the sudden sneeze made him stagger backwards.

"Cheers, Fatty," chortled Tommy, wrenching the ball back.

As he turned away from the spluttering and distraught Pete, Tommy saw the others standing a few feet away. Danny's fists were clenched, knuckles whitening. Darren and Carl stood either side. Globulous sobs hacked in Pete's throat and chest. Behind them Dean was backing off towards the concrete steps.

"Tom! Let's go! This is boring now!" he barked. His voice hid the fact that he noticed Danny's fists clench white.

"You didn't have to make Pete cry, you – you – bully!" shouted Danny, stepping closer. He trembled as he moved, angry beyond awareness. His only thoughts were of footballs and absent fathers. His throat burned as he screamed, "Give us our ball back or I'll smash your face in!"

Darren's and Carl's eyes widened in surprise. Pete's would have, but the sand and tears had mixed into a kind of cement that glued his shut. Tommy, initially shocked, gave his best couldn't-care-less shrug and tossed the ball as far as he could in the direction of the sea. It landed in the surf, lolling in the foam. As the tide drew back, preparing to wash in a new wave, it was buoyed up on the receding water and floated around to the other side of the rocks.

The boys watched it disappear around the edge in dismay. Tommy pushed past, elbowing Carl out of the way as he went, and ran to join his fellow bully on the steps. They ran up the concrete and away into the town, shouting obscenities back at the beach long after they were safely out of earshot.

Danny strode angrily towards the rocks.

"Leave it, Dan," choked Pete through sand and watery, just-open eyes.

Danny was not listening, consumed with thoughts of revenge and his own father. And the ball that Pete's father had given him. Imagined pictures of his own father playing kickabout with him in the garden of their old house formed in front of his anger, behind his eyes. There had been no parting present for Danny when his father went. Dad would be back, Mum said at first. Then, later, Dad had gone away, Mum said. Finally, she had to tell him that Dad was living somewhere else, with some*one* else. Nothing there of Dad. Nothing real. But the ball was real. It reminded Pete of *his* Dad. Danny could not – would not – leave it. Not so much for his friend, but for himself. It would be like forgetting.

He put his foot on the first rock. He called over his shoulder, "I'll get it!" and began climbing. He found his footing easily, his trainers gripping on the lower, bigger rocks. He soon heaved himself up to the top, negotiating a route between globs of green mush and strands of seaweed that clung to the surface underfoot. He looked down around him and back over his shoulder. Over on the far side, the rocks led down precariously to the other stretch of beach. Behind him, less than two metres below, his friends were waiting. Pete's eyes were streaming and red. Carl pointed at his watch, impatient. Darren's foot was on the first rock.

"Need a hand?"

Danny stretched his neck, searching. "Dunno yet, Daz. Can't see... Oh! There it is!"

The ball had bobbed around to a shallow crevice below the rock on which Danny was standing. They all knew that the water was considerably deeper there, the depth falling away around the front of the rocks. So, to avoid swimming fully-clothed, Danny flattened himself on his chest. Damp algae from the rock surface slimed his jeans and glued itself to his t-shirt. He elongated his arm as far as he could until the tendons felt taut and his shoulder ached. His elbow clicked. The skin on his fingertips tightened. Just inches away from the ball. It was partly wedged in the fissure, the water lapping and slapping the plastic. He pushed for purchase against the wet rock, edging forward. His head tipped over the edge. With his head and shoulders leaning over, he thought, his reach would traverse those few inches. His trainers scraped hard along the rock as he tipped ever closer. His fingertips brushed the ball as bobbed up on a swell. Just one more stretch. He held his breath. Blood pounded in his temples. Suddenly, like a magnet, his palm fixed onto the ball. He began to close his hand, to bring the ball in.

The other boys saw the wave roll in towards them in time to call out, but the rushing sound around Danny's ears drowned them out. Surf and spray flared up around him like white fire. In the span of a single towering splash, his feet were scrabbling. It was useless, like trying to cut glass with fingernails. Desperately, he drew up a knee. His foot failed, slipping his centre of gravity forward. In a sightless white moment, a claw of foam enclosed his body.

He plunged. Cool, dull, soft silence surrounded him. Blinding white surf gave way to sudden greyness and an ache at his temples. He felt the sea envelop him, felt something nudge his calves as he kicked in protest. He beat at the thickness with his arms, the ball forgotten. He beat at the frothy greyness. With each kick it became darker.

His lungs straining, his throat tight as he fought to hang on to the air inside him, Danny thought for a moment that he saw a face in chaotic water. A face belonging to arms that reached out and held him, supported him as he struggled to swim. It was a man's face, an old face. It was warm and familiar yet grey and distant. Was it – could it be – his father? Too old-looking, surely? Dad? Dad!

By the time the other boys – the bullies included – managed to haul him out of the water, only seconds had passed but Danny was unconscious. When he came round, his eyes opening on the dark shape of his mother silhouetted against the summer sun, all of the boys were standing together. The ball was tucked under Pete's arm.

Danny had swallowed a few mouthfuls of sea water. Apart from the vomiting, he recovered quickly, although Mother insisted on him going to bed early and an unnecessary home visit from the doctor. Dad sent a Get Well Soon card co-signed by Dorothy. Danny wondered who Dorothy was. Mum wouldn't tell him for years, and when she finally did he had worked it out for himself.

Daniel looked at the father, now grey and dry, who avoided his gaze. He felt comfortably detached. They had met maybe half a dozen times in recent years, and in his own way George had tried to make up for his invisibility during his son's childhood, but 'Dad' was still just a word.

"Anyway…" Daniel began. The sentence went nowhere.

George stirred his tea. "Have you heard of *Dignitas*?" he said.

"Um… yes, of course. We ran an article on them not so long back, when they were taking part in a public debate at the town hall."

"Article?"

"Yes, Dad. I'm assistant editor on a listings magazine. I *have* told you before."

"Oh, yes. I see." He really didn't.

"Anyway…"

"Yes?"

"You were saying. About *Dignitas*, the euthanasia people. They're based in Switzerland, where the law is pretty liberal about assisted suicide. What do you want to know?"

"About what?"

"*Dignitas*, Dad. *You* brought the subject up."

"Oh, yes." He gave a little smile. "Son, I have something to tell you."

He had never called Daniel 'son' before. Neither of them had felt that he had earned that right, only re-entering his son's life once he was well into adulthood. Daniel quickly connected the dots. It came as no surprise when George said, "Son, I am afraid I have to tell you that I am dying."

Daniel was unsure what to say. He didn't seem to feel the way that he anticipated that he might feel if his mother had said the same thing. But this was his father. He should feel *something*.

"What is it?" he said at last.

"Well, I was having a lot of headaches, especially in the morning. And then I started having difficulty thinking, finding the right words. I suppose that was never my strong suit anyway. All those years, all those things that I should have said to your mother but I never did. All the times I should have picked up the telephone to speak to you…" He shook his head, as if trying to rub the thought away.

"Brain tumour."

George looked at his son, his eyes wide and accusing. Was he just perceptive or callous? Was this resentment or the lack of any feeling? The flatness of his son's statement caught him for a moment.

"Yes, it is. In the cerebellum. It's quite big and has probably been growing for some time. It isn't really in a good place".

"Operable?"

George found it difficult to meet his son's steady gaze. "Not really, no," he said. "The doctors have been talking about surgery but radiotherapy is a more likely course of action. On that I am not keen. I like my hair too much". With that, he attempted a joke, running his hand over the powdery grey mass on his head.

"So… you're…" Daniel hesitated as it began to sink in. "You're going for… assisted suicide?" He felt the blood drain from his cheeks as he said it.

George reached into his jacket and pulled out a bulging leather wallet. He allowed himself a wry smile. "Well, I am not a brave man. I left you and your mother rather than summon the courage to try harder – I am self-aware enough to know that. For that, I am deeply sorry. To both of you".

"That's big of you". It was unnecessary but he felt compelled to say it anyway.

"Well, quite. So… to the point. I am indeed going to take a flight on a budget airline, drink stewed coffee and eat a plastic-wrapped muffin. I am going to disembark in Switzerland and meet at an agreed location on an agreed date with a representative of an organisation very much like Dignitas. From that point onwards, my fate is in his hands."

"Wait a minute. 'An organisation *like*…' As in 'not actually'? What is it? A budget version? The Kwiksave value suicide package?"

George made an arch with his hands and pressed his lips against his fingertips. "Very witty," he said. "No, this is a new venture for him. It is new technology that is designed to not only ease one's passing but… *ensure that we continue afterwards*". He said the last few words slowly, then sat back and sipped his tea.

Daniel laughed. "You mean, Dad, that this Swiss Doctor Death…"

"Irish, in point of fact".

"Whatever. He's got you thinking that, what, he's going to save your soul? Where? In a box?"

"In a manner of speaking, yes. I type in my answers to some key questions and enter an authorisation code on his laptop computer, and this releases the drugs into my system. At the same time, electrodes attached to my head will preserve my brain patterns and transmit them".

"What? *Transmit* them? In what? An e-mail?"

"I'm not actually that familiar with the interweb or radio frequencies, but I do know that it is far more exciting than that. I will not be moving in space, but I will be transmitted *through time*, leaving my body behind".

Daniel removed his glasses and pressed his knuckles against his closed eyelids. "In a time machine. A laptop time machine. Via e-mail".

George drained his tea. He placed the cup on the tabletop with a clean clink. "You could put it that way. He says he has transported himself like this, and merely seeks to help others to escape the finality of the end by using this machine to duplicate his experience. He has travelled back to places he finds familiar. Perhaps it is a chance for me to... look in on you, make up for things in some way".

Daniel leaned back in his chair and looked at his watch. He ran his fingers through his hair, trying to think. Time was ticking on. "Look, Dad," he said, "I have to be back at work, but I'll call them and say it's a family emergency or something. Which wouldn't be far from the truth, would it? Let me go and refresh our drinks and call work, then I'll be right back. Okay?"

George gently nodded his assent, amused at his son's flustering. He watched his son join the queue and stand in wait behind a pregnant woman arguing with a young boy who wriggled his hand out of hers. That could have been his own boy, years ago, with his mother, negotiating the tides and turns of an average day. But without him. He was an absent father and, he saw now, that his recent attempt to forge a relationship with his estranged son was futile. It was like trying to gently tease open a gate rusted shut over many years. Too little too late.

He thought of Dorothy, at home, oblivious to his plans, believing him to be on a business trip. She knew all about Daniel, of course, and had encouraged him to make that first contact with his adult child. Over at the coffee counter queue, Daniel stood with arms folded, his wallet tucked under his arm, staring at nothing in particular. At the table, George popped open his own wallet, and took out a slender white business card, the thin cardboard folded into a tiny triangle at one corner. He placed it neatly on the table, facing squarely so that Daniel would read it when he sat down.

George had planned the next stage of the conversation carefully. If only he could remember how to begin. It was going to end with him asking his only son to join him on his only trip to Switzerland, for his only appointment with death.

No. Better to leave things as they were. In any case, if it all went according to plan, he would see Daniel again soon. It was just a matter of when and where. Choosing the right moment could make all the difference to a fractured childhood. Maybe he might even manage to heal a few cracks, if not repair the entire break. Putting his wallet back in his jacket pocket, he stood, carefully and with great effort. He paused, to gather his breath and check for signs of dizziness. His head was clear.

When Daniel returned to the table, tray of cups and sugar sachets in hand, the first thing he noticed was the embossed white rectangle arranged as a miniature placemat.

The second thing he noticed was the empty chair opposite. He looked up, searched the kaleidoscopic crowd for a hint of an older man with grey hair. Puzzled, but somehow not surprised, he sat down, wondering whether to wait or return to work or what to do.

He picked up the card, held it between his thumb and index finger. It was a business card, offering euthanasia services to the terminally ill. The name on the card was familiar, and instantly Daniel knew how he knew the name. It was unusual, difficult to forget.

Ruskin Claverty.

GRUFFUDD'S DOG

Hands grabbed Rufus by the scruff of the neck and flung him through the door. So this was his punishment for chewing up that woman's bag. She shouldn't have left it on the floor in the first place. Just for *that* she wouldn't even take him out for a walk? The mongrel shrugged it off with a snarl. He cocked his leg and emptied his bladder against the closed metal door. That showed them. Rufus the mongrel didn't need them anyway. He was his own dog. He paced the walls of his cage for a few minutes, then flopped down on the floor.

Rufus nuzzled his nose between his front paws. He tried to get comfortable, but his blanket was too thin. There was only concrete underneath it, and it was cold. Apart from a few minutes spent with the woman with the chewy bag, he had spent most of the day lying on the floor, only getting up when a face appeared at the glass. Rufus' cage was clean and well-kept, but he wasn't allowed to touch the people. He could only say hello through a see-through wall. Whenever he could hear people come through the door at the far end of the corridor, he would get up from his bed, wag his tail and go up to the window, trying to get their smell. If they were a young family, he would jump up and down, showing off the best way he could. The people always smiled and said nice things, but usually they moved on to the next cage. Sometimes, they picked another dog to take home. Rufus knew when that happened because there would be one less howl joining in the chorus at night time.

For weeks, he tried. He would wag and pant and dance around desperately, do whatever it would take to get the humans to let him out. He would run and fetch balls, let the visiting humans pull him on a lead down the road, and generally do as much as he could to make them like him. Maybe he tried too hard. It always ended with him back in the cold cage, with the metal door clanging shut behind him. On days like that, he would join in the howls at night. "What am I doing wrong?" he would ask the night. There was never any answer, and he would curl up in the corner on the hard floor, staring at the lonely darkness.

After a while, Rufus stopped trying, and he greeted every human face with a glare. He would look at them with dull, grey eyes. His stare was a wall keeping them out. If they looked particularly stupid, he would growl. Why bother if they were only going to reject him anyway?

Rufus had been living at the rehoming centre for only a few months, but because he was a dog and dogs sometimes have short memories, it felt to him as if he had been there forever. No one ever took him home in any of the cars that he heard drive away, and he was hardly ever allowed out to play. No one even knew that his name was Rufus. The girls who fed him, stroked him, walked him and kept him in a cage, called him 'Billy'. That wasn't the right sound at all, but how could he tell them?

Most people don't know that dogs understand almost everything that they say. Not just 'sit', 'good boy' or 'fetch', but all those silly arguments and pointless conversations about the weather that people have. Dogs don't bother with that kind of thing when they talk to each other. They usually don't have much to say that couldn't be said better with a sniff or a growl. But sometimes, when they can be bothered, they have very important things to say to each other.

So there was Rufus, one night, settling down on his tatty thin blanket, nose between his paws, when the howling party started up again. A sweep of wind scattered leaves against the windows and the Jack Russell in the next cage howled so loudly it was if he was trying to rip open the world.

A breeze prickled the hair on his hackles. His ears stood to attention. There was someone else in the cage. Had the door been opened? Maybe he hadn't heard it above the sound of Howler next door. He stood up and turned around to face the door. It was closed now but standing in front of it was another dog. Rufus was startled. He bowed his head, letting his stood-to-attention shoulders show. He growled. But there was something about the other dog that calmed him down. Rufus hadn't heard him come in, but he did hear him when he spoke, and his voice was very calm, confident, commanding. It was clear who was the boss right away.

It was a bit difficult to miss him this other dog anyway. A big, loping Irish Wolfhound, he cast a big shadow over scruffy mongrel Rufus. He was used to light shining in through the food hatch at the back of his cage. It was comforting, especially at night when the other lights were dimmed.

"You're in my light," he snarled. He couldn't let himself give in *that* quickly.

"Oh, I'm sorry," said the Irish Wolfhound softly. He was quiet and stepped off to one side. He waited.

"Well, come and sit down then," said Rufus.

The bigger dog settled down next to Rufus, and gave him a sniff in greeting.

"Do you mind?"

"Sorry, just being polite. Just trying to show I'm not here to bite you or take your rag away."

"It's a blanket."

"Oh, yes. I can see now. Fine wool, I see."

"More like man-made pretend wool. Who are you, anyway?"

"Me? Oh, I'm just a stray, brought in off the streets. You're Billy, aren't you? I overheard the humans talking. It looks as if we're sharing tonight. I hope you don't mind. I would have brought you something, but..."

Rufus gave him a look. Then he looked more closely. The wolfhound's eyes swam with darkness. There seemed to be depths of wisdom in those eyes, and when he looked around the cage, the hard coldness of it didn't seem to bother him. It was as if he owned it, and made the place warmer. It reminded Rufus of a dim memory of another dog keeping him warm and safe a long time ago, when he was a puppy.

"I'm fine, thanks. Name's Rufus. They don't know *anything* out there."

"Do they know *why* you're here?"

"I expect so. They brought me in. I was on the streets for a while after… something happened. A family did pick me once, and I went home with them, but they didn't like me so they brought me back after a few hours. They didn't even let me stay the night. I don't know what they expected, but it wasn't me."

"That's bad luck."

"Even worse for their carpets and curtains."

"Don't worry. Someone else will pick you sooner or later."

"Doubt it. Don't care. They can stuff it. When people come round, I'm going to just lie here and give them the look. They usually go to another cage anyway."

They lay on the floor for a while. The wolfhound was finding it difficult to get comfortable, and seemed to be favouring one side of his body. As he circled to find himself a spot to lie down, Rufus noticed a clump of matted hair that barely hid a scar. The flesh had healed, but it was bumpy, like flesh bubbles, not smooth. The wolfhound settled down, with his damaged side out of Rufus' view.

"Hope you don't mind me mentioning, but that's an impressive scar. How'd you get it?" said Rufus.

The older dog said nothing. He seemed to be thinking about how to answer. The electric lights in the ceiling were turned down, and Rufus grew cold again. Two cages down the row, a young mongrel started whimpering.

"Do you want to hear a story?" asked the wolfhound.

"Not particularly," sighed Rufus.

"Well, where I come from it's traditional. When we meet another dog, we say hello the usual way, then we tell a story, a bit like a pleased-to-meet-you present. Especially as I couldn't bring you anything, you might like it."

"You are seriously deranged, but you're bigger than me. Do what you like."

The wolfhound got up, his back legs creaking with age. He wandered over to the corner and lapped lazily from the water bowl.

"Have you heard of a place called Wales?" he asked.

"Yes. Lots of hills and really boring sheep," said Rufus, as he circled his blanket. He clawed at it, trying to make a comfortable mound to lie on.

"Well, my story took place in Wales many hundreds of years ago."

Oh, here we go, thought Rufus. Still, nothing better to do. I'll pretend to listen. Scar or not, he'd have me in a fight, no problem. He settled down on his made-up cushion. "Okay, ready."

"Nine hundred years ago, all of England was ruled by a man called King John, but Wales was divided up into lots of little kingdoms. When one of the kings died, groups of men fought for the right to rule each kingdom. A man called Llewellyn ap Iorwerth took over the throne of Gwynedd. Not all of the Welsh leaders were loyal to the English King, but Llewellyn promised to support King John so that he could protect his land. In return, King John said that Llewellyn could marry his daughter Joan."

"Marry? You mean they paired up?"

"Yes, Rufus. That is the concept, I believe. May I continue?"

"So he paired up with a princess?"

"Not really," sighed the wolfhound. "Not all of his children were royal. Joan had a mother who was a commoner."

"Eh?"

"Like a mongrel."

"What's wrong with that?"

"Well, as charming as you are, my boy, good breeding counts for a lot. Humans place a great deal of value on pedigree breeds," the wolfhound said. As he spoke, his back straightened with pride. "Anyway, marrying Joan was a way to make sure that Llewellyn would help King John out when he needed it."

"Did it work?" Rufus asked. Although he didn't want to, he was becoming interested.

"Well, it did for a while but humans almost always get into some sort of fight about who is in charge of what territory sooner or later. Dogs do too, but we don't have wars over it. Anyway, this story isn't about that. King John's wedding present to Llewellyn and Joan was a great Irish wolfhound that they called Gelert.

In those days, men would go out hunting in the woods for their food. Even then, many men saw it as a sport, and Llewellyn very much enjoyed hunting. Gelert was the strongest and biggest dog in the kingdom, so Llewellyn trained him to become leader of the hunting dogs. Gelert was so powerful that he could smell the scent of a stag further away than any other dog. He would set off after it, with the dogs and huntsmen following behind. Sometimes this would lead them miles away and they would have to set up camp. On one occasion, the scent ended at the widest part of a very deep river. Without hesitating, Gelert threw himself into the water and swam against the current. It wasn't until he reached the other side of the river that he realised that he had lost the trail of the stag."

The wolfhound chuckled a little to himself before he continued, "Sometimes, he did get rather carried away. Every

214

time Gelert picked up a fresh scent, they would go further and sometimes they would be away for weeks at a time. This used to annoy Joan, because she was left behind, and it was worse after their son Gruffudd was born. So she made her husband build some hunting lodges all over the land so that the whole family would have somewhere to stay when the hunt was on.

When the family would go out hunting with Llewellyn's men, they would often end up camping by one of the lodges. Gelert always tagged along, and it was on these trips that Llewellyn could see how loyal Gelert was to him. Most humans don't realise this, but we dogs pick our masters very carefully. The family and all the people in Llewellyn's household treated Gelert well, so he was happy to stick around. He always got the best bones and scraps from the kitchen, and he was always welcome with everyone, whether it was the boys who tended the horses, the women who wove baskets, or the men who fought in battles. It was often said that he was as gentle as a puppy with everyone who was kind to his master and his household."

Rufus was expecting to hear a story about a warrior dog from ancient times. "So he was a bit of a wimp then," he said.

"No, far from it," replied the old wolfhound. If dogs were able to do such things, he would have winked. "Whenever anyone approached the family with violence or threatening words, Gelert would stand between them, his hackles standing as high as saplings. His would bare his strong white teeth that were wet and shiny from chewing the bones of deer and pigs. His growl was deep. Many people said that his growl rumbled so loudly that it made their stomachs hurt. Llewellyn was so impressed with this that he let Gelert sit by him when he was at the banquet table. The other dogs were so jealous, mainly because Gelert got the best scraps from the table. He was far tougher than the rest of the dogs, though, so they never said anything. He was leader of the pack, and anyway, if it wasn't for Gelert's superior hunting abilities, there wouldn't be any meat on the table in the first place. But no one loved Gelert more than the children. He would let them all pull on his ears and climb on his back, but there was one child above all who had Gelert's loyalty."

"Who was that then?" Rufus asked. He was interested again. He would never admit it to another dog, but lying in his cage night after night, the only thing he could dream about was being with a family with children. He couldn't imagine any better life than running through fields chasing a ball thrown by some little boy or girl, and having someone who would stroke his fur and scratch him behind the ears. He couldn't remember the last time a human did that for him.

"Joan and Llewellyn had two boys. Their eldest was called Gruffudd, and he was best friends with Gelert. The younger brother, Dafydd, was just a baby, but Gruffudd was a bit older. He learned to walk by grabbing on to Gelert's tail as he roamed about the great hall. Gelert didn't even mind when Gruffudd pulled his ears or pinch his mane. You might now know this, Rufus, but dogs who have been around children a lot know that they don't mean to hurt us. They're just learning about things when they tug our ears or poke us in the eye, so we try to be patient. It's not easy sometimes, but Gelert never minded. He loved his master and he loved his master's boy. Llewellyn could see that Gelert protected Gruffudd well, so he let him sleep by the boy's cot at night. He would guard him throughout the night, waking up whenever there was an unusual sound, ready to bare those teeth and let out that deep rumbling growl.

It was hard to separate the boy and dog and sometimes Llewellyn became angry when Gelert would not come to the hunt because he was so busy playing with Gruffudd."

"Why?" asked Rufus. "Isn't that what men want us dogs for? They *want* us to play with their children, surely?"

"Well, yes," said the old wolfhound, "but it was different in those days. Every dog had to work for his keep. Times were hard and all the food had to be hunted. There were no tins of meat or boxes of biscuits back then. If a dog didn't hunt, he wasn't much use to the household."

"If someone gave me the chance, *I'd* hunt all day. It'd be better than being stuck in this place."

"That's a good point. Gelert didn't realise that. He started to think that his only job was to protect Gruffudd. In fact, when Llewellyn shouted at him for not coming to the hunt, Gelert was bare those shiny white teeth and growl back at his master! Llewellyn nearly got rid of him because even a dog like Gelert should know his place and respect his master. But Llewellyn *did* realise that Gelert did know his place after all, it just wasn't the place that Llewellyn had intended. Although Llewellyn was a powerful and warlike man, the safety of his family was important to him. He needed to know that his sons would be safe whenever he was out hunting or protecting his land and property from his enemies. Eventually, one of the other dogs replaced Gelert as leader of the hunting pack, and Gelert was allowed to stay behind to protect Gruffudd, who was not yet even two years old. Joan and Llewellyn had so much confidence in Gelert that they would leave him with Gruffudd in the lodge whilst they were out hunting. Dafydd was still a baby, so Joan would need to take him with her to feed him, but they knew Gruffudd would be fine with the wolfhound to protect him."

"Great, they just left him to be a babysitter instead! Maybe I'll just stay here if that's what I'd end up doing with a family, " said Rufus with a sigh.

The old wolfhound nudged Rufus with his nose. Despite this kind gesture, there was a superior tone to his voice, as if he was comparing Rufus to Gelert. "Life for *some* dogs is never that simple, young mongrel. Later that autumn, when the leaves were brown and crisp like old paper, the new hunt leader, anxious to prove himself, had spotted a stag further up the valley. So, Joan and Llewellyn put Gruffudd to bed, left Gelert in charge of the boy and went out to join in the hunt. It was a cold night. As the fog came in closer to the lodge, Gelert huddled closer to the boy's cot…"

Most of the other dogs in the rehoming centre were asleep now. In the distance, Rufus could hear a terrier whimpering quietly, and the wind began buffeting the trees outside. It sounded like giant sheets flapping on a washing line. He watched as the old wolfhound paused, then said, "It was a night like tonight, only much colder. Llewellyn didn't return until late that night, but he was in a good mood. They had hunted the deer and trapped a few rabbits along the way. There would be enough for a banquet the following day. He was looking forward to sharing his good fortune with his eldest son and his loyal dog, but his warm joy suddenly faded and became cold when he saw the door to the lodge. It was open, swinging creakily in the wind.

Llewellyn ran into the lodge, straight into the main hall. Tables and benches were overturned, one of them splintered as if a heavy weight had barged into it. His first thought was that one of his enemies had broken in to steal gold and tapestries, but he noticed quickly that nothing was missing. He clenched his jaw and drew his sword. Holding it in front of him, ready to swing its blade into dark corners, he ran through the hall. On the far side were his private rooms, one of which was Gruffudd's bed chamber. Shouting and roaring to scare away his enemy, he burst in to the room.

The first thing he saw was his son's cot. It lay on the floor, broken. The sheets and furs on which Gruffudd slept soundly every night spilled out from the crib which lay on its side. Spots of blood stained the ripped and crumpled sheets. The corner of one sheet was soaking up blood from a deep red pool on the stone floor. Llewellyn's eyes darted from the heavy cot to the floor and around the room. His son was nowhere to be seen. The only living thing was Gelert, who peeked out at his master from behind the overturned cot.

Gelert was matted with blood, and streaks of red mixed with the grey and black hair of his muzzle. His jaws were stuck with blood. With his head bowed, he looked up at his master nervously.

It was obvious to Llewellyn what had happened.

With a great cry of pain and anger from deep within his stomach, Llewellyn raised his sword high above his head, his eyes firmly on Gelert's bloody face. With one movement that split the air, Llewellyn thrust his sword deep into the dog's side. It went in under the ribs, slicing into Gelert's body.

The great dog's howl ripped the night apart. All the dogs in the hunting pack knew that it was a howl of sadness and regret. He was wounded so badly that he could barely stand. With his eyes, he tried to explain to Llewellyn, but it was no use. He fell to the floor like a bag of stones.

Llewellyn's heart and brain fought with themselves inside his body. He trembled with anger and fear that the dog that he trusted so much had betrayed him, murdering his beloved son. But his love for Gelert was almost as strong as his fatherly love for Gruffudd, and his eyes filled with tears of regret. His sword fell to the floor with a crash and a clatter, like a breaking window. Without thinking, he fell to his knees, reaching out to Gelert's heaving flank.

Just as his fingers touched the dog's trembling shoulder, he heard a noise. There was a cough and a snuffle, muffled and struggling. Llewellyn let out an enormous groan of rage that was loud enough to rattle bones. With a heave, he lifted the broken cot and pulled at the heavy fur blankets and bloodstained sheets. Safe and warm under the pile of bedding was Gruffudd, barely breathing frightened, but still alive.

But that was not all. There was something underneath Gruffudd. A struggle had brought boy, blankets and cot down on top of something. Something that was now dead. As Llewellyn clutched the boy close to his chest, small arms wrapped around his neck, he looked down at the dead body of the largest wolf that he had ever seen.

Where the wolf's throat should have been was a ragged, torn hole from which blood had poured onto the floor. The wolf's head lay in a dark red pool that was growing thick and sticky. With a sob that shook the hardened warrior more than anything ever before, Llewellyn realised the truth. He had made a terrible mistake.

Cradling his son in the crook of his arm, he kneeled beside his faithful dog, as the wolfhound's breathing became slow and quiet. With his other hand, he gently gathered Gelert's head into his lap.

Gelert tried to lick his master's hand but he no longer had enough strength to lift his head.

Tears fell from Llewellyn's eyes and mingled with the blood on Gelert's muzzle. Llewellyn stroked the dog's head and scratched him gently behind the ear. Gelert half closed his eyes with pleasure.

The only words that Llewellyn could whisper were, "I'm sorry."

Even with the pain deep inside him from his master's sword, Gelert knew what the words meant. He could see that his young master was safe. A touch from his old master was the only thing that he needed know. Llewellyn stroked his head one last time.

With a shudder, Gelert released his last breath. Both father and son watched as the great dog's eyes changed. Where they were deep rivers, now they were dark glass.

Llewellyn realised that the wolf had come into the lodge looking for food. It tore apart the great hall, but found nothing to eat. Somehow, it had found its way to Gruffudd's bed chamber, but it hadn't expected to meet Gelert. The great warrior wolfhound had fought the wild wolf with all of his strength, fuelled by his love and loyalty for Gruffudd. It was a battle to the death. In the struggle, the cot and blankets had been pulled down on top of the wolf, with Gruffudd caught up in the bedding. But Gelert had the wolf by the throat, and with one bite of his powerful jaws, he killed the wild animal. He had saved Gruffudd's life.

Llewellyn buried Gelert in open land by the river Glaslyn, where the wind would sweep and carry the howl of hounds down the valley for miles. Even as Gruffudd grew older and memory of his faithful nursery companion grew distant, Llewellyn's grief grew ever stronger. A year later, Llewellyn put up a memorial stone by Gelert's grave. It can still be seen today. The nearby village is called Beddgelert – Gelert's Grave."

If dogs could cry, the Irish Wolfhound's eyes would be brimming with tears. He stared into the distance at the end of his story, as if he'd forgotten that Rufus had been listening. Rufus looked at the glass of their cage. Their reflections stared back, like ghosts.

"That's quite a story," said Rufus eventually.

"Yes, it is," agreed the wolfhound. He got up, went over to the water bowl, lapped up a drink, then padded back. He sat, facing Rufus. Rufus pulled himself up so that they were almost face to face. He couldn't quite manage it because the wolfhound was quite a bit taller than him.

There was a pause.

"What?" said Rufus.

"I said nothing."

"I know! You're just, what, *looking* at me? You don't have to show me who's boss. I'll roll over if you like."

"I am wondering."

"Wondering what?"

"I am wondering what you think of the story."

"Uh… I've never been asked that kind of question before. I mean, we dogs pass on things we know about other dogs, but…"

"Tell me."

"Fine. Well, um, I think Gelert was *stupid*. He got killed protecting a kid that was going to forget him anyway, and Llewellyn didn't even give him a chance."

"Well, that's family for you. Fathers and mothers usually put their children first, and sometimes that stops them from thinking clearly. But I doubt that Gruffudd forgot him. Children remember *everything* in their *hearts*, even if some of it gets pushed to the backs of their heads. It's the same with us, isn't it?"

Rufus thought about this for a moment. Like most dogs, he very much lived in the present. There were things about his life before he ended up on the streets that he couldn't remember, and there were things that happened to him that he had been trying to forget, but he *did* remember the smile and the smell of the old lady who he lived with for a while. Maybe that was why he wanted a new home so much. Unfortunately, the wolfhound had reminded him of what happened all those months ago.

Rufus had been born on the dirty floor of a barn. The first sounds that he remembered hearing were other dogs whimpering. Some were mothers in pain, some were puppies calling for their mothers. It was some time before he could open his eyes to see his surroundings. To begin with, his world was the warmth of his mother and the tumbling, twisting bodies of his brothers and sisters. They would climb over each other, hungry for their mother's milk. Gradually, there were fewer little bodies sharing his mother, and eventually there was no mother. The first thing that Rufus remembered seeing was a pair of hairy human hands reaching down towards him. There was dirt under the fingernails. Bare electric light from the roof of the barn reflected off the rings on the human's fingers.

The first two years of Rufus' life were spent mostly indoors, either huddled with the other dogs in the cold of the barn, or later in the back of the pet shop. At the least the cage that he was in now was bigger than that one.

The pedigree dogs all found homes before Rufus, but the old lady who took him home with her one day gave him the best home of all. She fed him well, and he slept at the foot of her bed every night. Her grandchildren visited every day and the smallest one, mop-haired Joe, helped teach Rufus to empty himself outside rather than in the house. Once he learned, Rufus was surprised that it had never occurred to him before. The smells certainly improved.

"Rufus? I'm not accustomed to mongrels not listening to me," the wolfhound barked.

Rufus looked up at him, his eyes sparkling with memory. "Sorry," he said. "I was remembering something."

"Do you know how Gelert felt about his master?" It was a very direct question. The wolfhound seemed to know what Rufus was thinking.

"Not really, but I want to. I nearly did once but it didn't last long."

"Do tell me, young mongrel. What happened?"

Rufus concentrated hard. He had buried the memory for so long. "There was this old human. I lived with her for a while. Not more than a few moons had passed, then one morning she didn't wake up. I stayed with her, keeping her warm, until her son came. He said nothing to me, just took me in a car to a field. He threw a ball for me into the long grass. I went for it. By the time I had it in my teeth, he was gone. I tried to find my way back, but I was in a confusing new place. Whenever I tried to ask a human for help, I would get shouted at or pushed away. I don't know how long I was sleeping under trees or tipping bins over for my dinner, but eventually some humans put something round my neck and brought me here."

The wolfhound nodded, saying nothing.

Rufus lay down again, his jaw resting on his paws. "I hate humans. Every time I give them a chance, they sling me back in a cage. So I'm not giving them any more chances. I'm not jumping up and down for them anymore."

"Perhaps they are not all the same. Perhaps you are judging them too soon. Think about how they see *you* when you do that. Llewellyn misjudged Gelert, but Gelert knew that it was because of his love for Gruffudd and, in the end, Llewellyn proved his love for Gelert as much as Gelert proved his loyalty to his master. Gelert always kept his trust in the humans, and that is what will make his story last for ever."

"It *would* be good to have a human to look after like that," said Rufus. Suddenly, the wolfhound looked very tired to him, as if telling the story had taken al his energy away.

"All you have to do is let them trust you," said the old wolfhound. "Time for us to sleep, I think."

Rufus agreed, and the two dogs settled down, curled up against each other, on the thin grey blanket. Warm and comfortable, Rufus closed his eyes and dreamed of chasing rabbits through open fields.

Morning came with the clang and clatter of metal food bowls hitting the concrete floor, followed by the pattering of dried food. Rufus opened his eyes, yawned and stretched. He sniffed the air. His breakfast was ready. With a wag of his tail, he went over to his bowl and chomped down. One of the girls patted him on the head. "Good boy, Billy," she said. Just for once, he didn't mind.

Rufus didn't realise he was alone until he had finished his food. Licking the last morsel off the tip of his snout, he looked around. His new cellmate was gone. No Irish Wolfhound, not one hair. Even his smell seemed to have faded away.

There was a tap on the window. Without thinking, Rufus bounded over, wagging his tail at the boy on the other side of the glass. He must have been about eight years old. The boy waved enthusiastically at Rufus, then turned to his father and pointed. Rufus pressed his nose up against the barrier and the boy spoke to him. "Hello, boy," he said. "Do you want to come home with us?"

Rufus wagged his tail furiously.

"Steady," said the boy's father. "We need to check him out first and get to know him a little."

No problem, thought Rufus. The boy looked into his eyes. They were like deep rivers.

THE LYREBIRD ON THE DOORSTEP

Neomie sat on the back step, frowning. She kicked her scuffed sneakers in the dust, her jeans dragging with the heels. A pebble took to the air, flicked up by Neomie's toe. She imagined that it was aimed at her mother.

Beyond the end of the garden, the Yarra Valley opened up like a split melon, spreading out all the wildlife of Victoria like seeds. The sights and sounds of the bush seemed to go on forever. Infinite blues and greens stretched away into the forest. It was so different from what she would see and hear every day back in Melbourne. It was a new life and a new world of platypus, koalas, emus, wombats and eagles.

Before the family moved out this way, Neomie would dream about seeing the birds and animals that her parents told her about, and that she only saw in books or on television. In her dreams, she would fly with the eagles and climb trees with the koalas. The reality was a little different. Eagles were scary and koalas slept a lot. Boring, boring, boring!

No friends, no school yet, no shopping malls. No TV, no Internet, *no life!* Everything still in boxes, Mum and Dad too busy to even talk half the time, ten-year-old Neomie was sent to play outside. Where? Play what? Who with? She couldn't even e-mail her pen friend in England. School had set that up, a project for sharing experiences in different countries. After all her friends had got bored with it, Neomie still carried on. For Neomie and slightly older English girl Hannah Partridge, the language of boredom was universal. Neomie wanted to scream out loud. Instead, she kicked up pebbles.

There was only a week to wait until Neomie would be able to start her new school, but it was a week too long. Ten was an age where the time between breakfast and afternoon was, well, *ages*. Never mind a week!

Neomie scooped up a handful of pebbles and, one by one, bounced them off the bark of the nearest tree. The last pebble sailed past the trunk and skittered into the undergrowth.

"Careful!" a thin voice called out.

She looked up to see where the sound came from. Nobody around. There was no one peeking out of bushes. There was no one sitting on a rock. There was no one waving hello. Neomie was puzzled. Maybe she dreamed it. Maybe her mind wandered off into a daydream. She wouldn't be surprised if she had. There wasn't much else to do on her own.

Neomie listened hard to see if she could hear the voice again. Just beyond the low fence and lush ferns at the end of the garden was the wildlife sanctuary, which surrounded the family's new home. It was where Mum and Dad worked, and it was full of its own sounds that wove in and out of the air like a musical picture. A chorus of frogs croaked their news to each other, and an orchestra of birds chirped and tooted and sang over the buzz and chatter of insects.

Neomie missed the hoot of horns and the revving of engines that she would hear from the road outside her bedroom window back in Melbourne. All her parents ever wanted to talk about now was the animals. All that she wanted, more than anything, was to leave the buzzing insects behind and return to the city, with her friends, her school, her shops.

Suddenly, from behind the tree, a bird appeared. It was a blur, diving into the undergrowth like a seal into water.

Neomie called out, "Hello!"

No answer. There was a rustle, and a little head peeped out from behind a gum tree. It was a teardrop on its side, with a thin pointed beak and black, open eyes. The rest of the bird emerged from its hiding place, its tail feathers fanned out. The wispy feathers riffled as it strutted towards Neomie.

High above, Neomie heard something chirrup. In front of her, the fanned-out bird repeated the same sound, like an echo but closer instead of further away. It strutted out of the grass, its pointy bird feet crunching the gravel that led up to Neomie on the back step.

"G'day, bird," said Neomie.

Time seemed to stand still, as if Neomie was suddenly inside a photograph. "G'daybird," replied the bird. Or did it? Was it some other sound? Did Neomie just imagine it?

Neomie felt her scalp prickle. This was weird. The bird splayed out his plumes of feathers and twittered, cawed and whooped. It cocked its head and shook its tail, fanning out over its back. It opened its beak wide and made a rising falling tone that sounded exactly like a car alarm going off. Neomie's father's car alarm, in fact. Next was a buzzing that ended in a spluttering tick-tick-tick. Was that a chainsaw?

"Holy Dooley!" Neomie whispered. She had heard her Dad say that. In fact, it was one of his favourite expressions. Now seemed the right time to use it herself.

The bird seemed to look at her quizzically.

"How did you…?" she began.

The bird let out a croak like a frisky frog and strutted off, disappearing back into the forest.

Neomie spent most of the afternoon scouring the trees and bushes, looking for the bird. No such luck.

Over dinner, after Mum and Dad had exhausted their tales of bandaging injured wombats and lecturing ungrateful pommies on local wildlife conservation, Neomie told them about the bird.

Dad leaned back in his chair, gathering his hair back behind his head with his hands. He had the same dark mop as Neomie, with little kinks and curls here and there. "A chainsaw, you say?"

"Yeah, Dad. Fair dinkum! It was like the real thing, right there in front of me!" she said, her eyes widening with the wonder of it all.

Dad smiled. He liked it when Neomie was enthusiastic about animals. It was what he did all day, look after animals, and it was satisfying to see his daughter starting to see what was so good about it. "Do you know what bird it was?" he asked.

"No," she said, "but it was kind of dark, with these spread-out feathers in its tail."

"Sounds like you met a lyrebird. They're amazing mimics. They copy all the sounds they hear in the forest, sometimes to attract a mate, other times to avoid predators. I came across one once, me and Bill Millwood were taking photos in the forest, and we thought we could hear another photographer. We could hear the shutter closing, even the motor on the camera. We turned around, and there it was, the flamin' bird! Making camera noises, it was." He smiled at the memory. Bill Millwood was his best friend, who had died a few months earlier. That was why the family had moved here, to help run the visitor's centre at the wildlife sanctuary, after Bill passed away.

"Wow."

Dad leant forward again and took a forkful of his food. Mum had been sitting at the table with them, but had eaten quietly, not talking much to Neomie. Now, she was getting up from the table with her plate, off to the compost bin with her scraps. Dad took the chance. "You need to talk to Mum," he said.

"Why?"

"You upset her this morning, arguing about this place." He waved his fork around to vaguely indicate that he meant where they now lived. Not Melbourne.

"Is she… Will she be angry with me again?"

"Nah, she'll be apples, but you need to talk to her. Now." He jabbed the fork in the direction of the back door, where Neomie could see her mother in the garden. Although she didn't really understand why, Neomie knew that she was more like her father than her mother. She looked more like Dad, she talked more like Dad, and Mum said she even thought more like Dad. How did Mum know what was going on in her head?

Mum was watering plants with an old metal watering can. Her fair hair was blonde with a tint of red that hinted at the copper-coloured hair of her own mother. It was long and frizzy, tied back but long strands hung over her face. Neomie wanted to go and tuck them behind her mother's ears, but she was afraid that Mum would think she was trying to pull her hair. Mum often misunderstood what Neomie was trying to say. She thought that Mum didn't want to listen. Dad said that the two of them just spoke different languages.

Neomie stood on the same back step where she had sat earlier that day. She felt ashamed when she remembered pretending to throw stones at her mother. Mum looked up from her gardening.

"Mum," she began.

"Yes, Neomie?" Mum was still annoyed.

"Sorry, Mum."

"What for?"

"For earlier." Obviously.

"Why?"

This is what made Neomie angry. Mum wouldn't let her just say it and get it over with. She always wanted her to *explain*, and say it the *right* way. Neomie rolled her eyes. She took a deep breath and said the words that she knew Mum wanted to hear because she had made her say them so many times before. "I'm sorry for saying what I said. I didn't mean it when I said I hate you. I was just annoyed because I'm so bored and I wanted to go to the shops and you said no because it's too far away and you had to work."

"That's all right, Neomie. If you go and do the dishes with Daddy now you could have some ice cream when you've finished." Mum turned off down the garden and carried on watering.

Neomie stood for a moment. Did Mum actually listen to what she said? Especially the bit about being bored?

There was a flutter somewhere among the trees. Neomie's eyes darted to where she thought the sound was coming from. Was that the lyrebird again? What was that sound? She held her breath so that it wouldn't drown out the faintest sounds and she concentrated hard with her ears. Was that a croak? Was there a "hello" amongst the chirps and chirrups?

That evening, Neomie and her father watched television together. Mum popped in now and again, to chat or to bring them drinks. The rest of the time she spent in the room that she called her studio, painting. Mum liked painting wildlife, watercolours mostly. She had even sold a few back in Melbourne. Finding new things to paint was one of the other reasons for moving out to the valley. She had been working on a new painting for a few days, but Neomie wasn't allowed to go in the studio. That had been one of the other reasons for the argument that morning.

As Neomie drifted off to sleep later that night, she listened to the sounds of the forest change. Different animals called out to each other in the darkness. Before she fell asleep, she wondered whether they called out because they were gathering all their friends together for a party or whether it was because they were lonely.

*   *   *

Neomie was sitting on the step again, but this time it was different. The sky above was a creamy blue and the light shining through the trees seemed to be tinged with vanilla.

Like a parting curtain, the green leaves in the undergrowth made way for the lyrebird. It strutted out, then stopped in front of Neomie. It flashed its fan of tail feathers like a magician showing off his cards before tucking them away again. *For my next trick...* thought Neomie.

"Hey," said Neomie.

"Hey," said the bird.

"You spoke!"

"Yep."

"How?"

"Well, there's a question. Sure you want to know?"

"Yes!" Neomie was so excited she didn't even notice that she was no longer sitting on the step but crouching down beside the lyrebird.

"First of all, let me ask you a question," said the bird. It was weird. His beak didn't move much. The sound of words just sort of came out, as if he had a speaker inside him.

"Okay."

"Where are we now?"

"In the garden." She looked around as she said it, noticing that there seemed to be a few extra shades of green since this morning.

"Yes and no. This is the Dreamtime."

Neomie remembered learning something about this at school, something about it being to do with Aboriginal culture. It was maybe even *everything* to do with Aboriginal culture, an entire history, but she wasn't sure.

"The what?" she said.

"The Dreamtime," replied the bird.

"I mean, what is it?"

"Well, it is the story of things that have happened. It is also the story of how the universe and everyone in it were created and how everyone is meant to work together."

"Are we in a story, then?"

"Yes, if you like."

"I must be dreaming."

The lyrebird didn't answer. He paraded back and forth, occasionally pecking at the earth. Neomie waited. Everything around her was so different. She felt as if she were standing in a painting of the garden rather than the garden itself. Colours shimmered, as if stirred by hidden winds.

Eventually, the lyrebird spoke. "Dreamtime is the time before time, when all things were made."

"Then how can I be in it? I'm only ten."

"You are seeing the edge of it as part of your Dreaming. I am your Ancestor Spirit. Once, most of the spirits slept in the earth until The Father of All Spirits sent the Sun Mother to wake us. When she did, she sent out her heat and light and gave us forms. Some of us are the trees, the plants, the flowers. Some of us are the animals, the insects, the fish. Some of us are…"

"Birds?"

"Yep. This is your Lyrebird Dreaming."

Neomie looked around her, at the brushstrokes of the trees and the stippled leaves. It made sense, sort of. And she wasn't afraid.

"I can understand you. Is that because I'm just imagining it?"

The lyrebird's neck stiffened. He looked at her sharply, as if hurt. "There is a difference between the Dreaming and making things up. This should be as real to you as anything else, if you know how to listen."

Neomie looked at the ground, her toe scraping a line in the dirt. "Mum doesn't think I listen either," she mumbled. "Dad says it's like we speak different languages."

The lyrebird spread his wings, freeing his feathers with a shake. Tucking them back in, he said, "In the Dreamtime, in the time before time, all the animals and birds spoke the same language. There were no arguments, because every animal or bird understood each other. There was so much food to go

242

around that there was no need for any animal to hunt another animal. Every animal got along well, and even danced the corroberee, where they would paint designs on their bodies and share information from the Dreaming.

One day, all the animals decided to hold the biggest corroberee that had ever been seen. Every flying fauna, crawling creature or slithering species was invited. They all rehearsed their parts in the dance. The Yellow-Faced Whip Snake practised his turn with the laughing Kookaburra, long before the snake would become the cackling bird's food.

The best dancing bird in the land, the Brolga, put himself in charge of the dancing. He always put himself in charge, that one. He would pirouette and prance with everything he did, even when he was just going to the water hole."

The lyrebird seemed to shrug, as if irritated by the thought of the brolga. Neomie felt a bit uncomfortable, so she reached out to stroke his head. He jerked away. She withdrew her hand, embarrassed.

"I'm sorry," she said. "It just seemed like… You sound like you know the bird that you're talking about. He sounds a bit up himself."

"Yes, well, he *was*. And I did know him. If you're patient, you'll see that this story is about *me*. It is *my* Dreaming." The lyrebird leaned in to Neomie's hand and nudged it with his head. "You can stroke me if you want. I'm just not used to it."

Neomie patted the bird gently with her fingers. "What did you do at the carib – corrib –"

"Corroboree. It was like a huge party. Big-headed brolga was boss of the dancing, like I said, and the Dingo and Kookaburra were going to sing. I didn't have any particular plans. I thought I'd just show off my tail feathers and join in. After all, I was hosting the party. All the animals gathered at the water hole beside my nest. They all came. First were the birds: the Crow, the Eagle, the Galah, the Kookaburra; then came the Wombat, the Frog, the Platypus; the Kangaroo and Wallaby arrived last. They always like to bound in, those two, making an entrance. In the Dreamtime, your ideas of future and past don't work quite the same way, but none of us could remember having been to a party as big as this one before.

We had a great time. We cringed at the Kookaburra's stupid jokes. She thought they were the funniest things ever. She laughed so loudly that the Koala was shaken from his tree. He landed with a bump, but curled himself into a ball and went back to sleep. Koalas are like that. No one else laughed as much as the Kookaburra. Rather full of herself, she was. In fact, some of us laughed *at* her, rather than *with* her, especially the Frog.

The Frog, who always did have a cheeky side to him, decided to mimic the Kookaburra's voice, He got everything exactly right, all the irritating notes in her voice, and told jokes that were far funnier than hers. Even though many of us had heard them before, we thought it was hilarious. I admired his bravery, because the Kookaburra could be quite prissy when it suited her, but she took it well and laughed even louder. He was a good mimic, that Frog. Such innocent times, when we could cavort around like that.

After that, the Brolga danced. We all just stood back and watched to begin with. The Brolga was the rightful master of the art of dance."

"What's a brolga?" asked Neomie.

The lyrebird tossed his head as if offended, but he was too polite to show it. "You don't know much about us birds, do you, young lady?" he said.

Neomie shifted uneasily, drawing a line guiltily in the dust with her toe. "Well, I'm from the city…"

"Hmm. Well, the Brolga is a large grey crane, much bigger than me. With his featherless red head and grey crown, he carried himself as if he were the king of the birds. In a way, he was. What he could do with those feet and his spindly legs would put any dancer to shame. He would trumpet 'Garoo' or

'Kawee-kree-kurr-kurr' whilst spinning or leaping in the air. Yes, the Frog could do that, but usually when the Brolga wasn't looking. After a while, we couldn't hold back any longer and had to join in. All the animals and birds began dancing, some trying to follow the Brolga's moves, others doing their own thing. Some just stumbled and fell over. Not every animal is made for dancing, unfortunately. But we were all too polite to tell the stout and sturdy Wombat that he wasn't as graceful as the Brolga. His stubby legs made him a great digger but not so good when trying to pirouette.

The Frog, who was never very tactful at the best of times, thought that the Wombat looked hilarious, stomping clumsily next to the Brolga, so he had an idea. Now, the Frog isn't really a bad animal, he just got carried away, caught up in the merriment and the fun. He copied the Brolga's voice, and, hiding in the crowd, told the Wombat that he looked fat, stupid, and clumsy, and that his dancing was a joke. He actually was all of those things, but nobody likes to be told that kind of information. Up to this point, the Wombat had looked up to the Brolga, but now he stopped what he was doing and glared at the Brolga, who had no idea that his fat friend was upset at him. This only made the Wombat angrier. How dare the Brolga talk to him like that! Not even the Crows would be that insulting!

The Frog was so pleased with himself that his trick worked that he tried it on another animal. I should have tried to stop him, but he hid himself in the long grass near to the Emu, who was trying to leap like the Brolga. Of course, as the Emu is a flightless bird, she was finding this difficult. Pretending to be the Brolga again, the Frog's voice took on a mocking tone and said, 'Dance, Emu? You can't even fly!' The Emu was so embarrassed that she wanted to hide her head in the sand until it was all over. Unfortunately, most of the other animals could hear it as well. In the chaos of everyone dancing and laughing, no one could be sure that the Brolga wasn't actually speaking. The Emu looked at her small wings, and she started to twitch with anger. I could see what was coming, but I couldn't get to the Emu quickly enough. By the time I had flapped my own wings twice, she had rushed headfirst at the Brolga.

That Frog just didn't know when to stop. There was me, shouting at him to be quiet, but too many of the other animals hadn't yet noticed. They couldn't see him, as he stayed hidden. I discovered later that he had crept behind a eucalyptus tree, where Koala might have noticed if he had been up there, but he was still sleeping on the ground. He had already used up more energy than he normally would. Even as the Emu started pecking furiously at the Brolga, the Frog started jeering. He called out all kinds of impolite comments, his voice disguised as the Kangaroo and the Kookaburra. He pretended to be the Eagle and insulted the Platypus. 'Hey, Platty!' he said. 'Why do you look like two animals stuck together? You look like a duck pie!', which hurt Platypus' feelings immensely. She was already sensitive about her shape, like the Wombat. Frog made up a song for the Wombat, which he sang in the Kangaroo's voice. Admittedly, it was quite catchy. It went, 'Roly-poly-foly-woly Wombat ate a dozen grubs and then a bat'. But no one else sang along.

I looked frantically for the Frog, but I couldn't find him. In the meantime, all the other animals blamed each other and started throwing insults all over the place. The Snake and the Cat pulled the Emu and Brolga off each other, but not before the Emu had damaged the Brolga's leg. He had to stand on one leg to rest his knee, which the Emu had pecked and pecked until it bled.

I spotted the Frog behind the tree. He was laughing, enjoying the spectacle of feather and fur flying all around him as the animals and birds fought all around him. Even the Koala joined in when he was woken up by the Frog calling him a lazy lump. He thought it was one of the Crows cawing in his ear.

Suddenly, the Frog leapt up. Still, no one noticed that it was he who called out, "Fight! Fight! Fight! Last one standing is an Earthworm!' As you can imagine, this didn't please the Earthworms much at all.

I headed straight for that mischievous Frog, but he jumped up out of my reach onto a tall rock, where he could look down on the chaos. I spread out my tail feathers to get everyone's attention. Normally, my feathers are so beautiful that I can't be ignored…"

Neomie felt she should interrupt at this point to agree with him, out of politeness at least. "Well, they *are* quite pretty," she said.

The lyrebird looked at her, his eyes hard glittering beads in the strange light. "Of course. Now, if I may continue, there *is* a point to this story."

"Sorry."

"All right then." He fanned his feathers, shook them, then tucked them back in, as if to emphasise his point. "I fanned my feathers and ran from animal to bird to animal again, trying to tell them it was the Frog's fault. I pleaded with them to stop, but either they couldn't hear me above the growling, screeching and squeaking, or they didn't want to listen. There were other animals that were far more important than me. It went on and on."

"How did it stop?" asked Neomie.

"The fighting and arguing got worse and worse and louder and louder. The air was so full of noise that the Wind went away to the open spaces beyond the forest, and I found it difficult to flap my wings to reach the Frog. He was urging them on and on, until suddenly the sky filled with new shades of colour. The noise had woken the Spirits."

Neomie had never heard the like. "Wow," she said. "Fair dinkum?"

"Yes. They stopped the fighting and made us all stand still. They were very angry indeed and we were all very embarrassed."

"What are they like?"

"Who?"

"The Spirits."

"Well, they're Spirits."

"I've never seen one."

"Oh yes, you have. You just don't know it. The Spirits are Now, Then and Soon. They are Sky, Sea and Sleep. They are visible and invisible, with you but alone." As the bird said this, he looked up at the sky, as if recalling a lost sad memory.

"Oh." Neomie thought she understood, but she wasn't sure. It was probably better to let the bird continue.

"The Sprits decided to punish us. We had always been able to talk to each other and understand each other, but the Spirits took that away because of the fighting. We lost our common language. From that moment onwards, each animal and bird spoke its own language. Dogs would only understand other dogs; wombats would only understand other wombats. Some animals kept the beauty of their original voices, particularly the birds. If you listen to the forest, you can hear us birds calling out to each other. We enjoy each other's music, but only a crow knows what another crow is saying, and it's the same with the kookaburra and... Anyway, that isn't so bad. But I did feel sorry for the Frog, even after all the trouble he caused."

"What did they do to him?" Neomie was desperate to know.

"That naughty Frog. His own voice had been so beautiful, and he was so skillful at copying other voices. It was such a sad loss."

"What happened? Tell me!"

If the lyrebird could have shaped his beak into a smile, he would have. She could tell he was teasing her. "Have you ever seen a frog?"

"Yeah, loads!"

"What sound do they make?"

A light went on is Neomie's head. "They croak!"

"Exactly! The Spirits punished Frog by giving him a croak. There would be no more singing and mimicking for him. It always sounds now as if it is painful for him to even call out to his friends."

The lyrebird looked modestly at the ground. It almost seemed that he was ashamed. Neomie had seen him show so much pride in himself up to this point. "What about you?" she asked. "What was your punishment?"

He looked up. "Punishment? Oh no, Neomie. I was given a *reward*. Because I was the only animal who had tried to stop the fighting, they decided to make me the only animal that would still be able to talk to all the others. Apart from me, no animal or bird can talk to one of a different kind. They can only talk to their own. And now, outside of the Dreamtime, in the world of people and gardens and cities, I am the only animal able to talk to all the other animals. I can imitate their voices. And other sounds too. I am always there in the forest, ready to talk peace between animals, ready to listen, ready to answer the call of the loneliest of all animals. That's why the original people of this land respect me as a peacemaker."

Neomie wondered which animal was the loneliest of all. Then she realised. Every animal is lonely at some time or another. And so is every person. But it was OK, because there is always someone to listen, whether it is a person, or an animal, or a bird.

"Do you ever get lonely, Mister Lyrebird?" she asked.

He hesitated. "There is always an ear to hear me, whether it's of my kind or another," he said. "You're never lonely as long as there is someone to listen to you, and no one is ever lonely if *you* listen to *them*. Remember, *listening* is different from *hearing*. You just need to learn to speak the same language."

Neomie thought of her mother and of that morning. She remembered what Dad had said. She and Mum *just spoke different languages.* She suddenly remembered something. The step. Where was it? She looked around, trying to find the step and the door to the house. Everywhere she turned there were trees, bushes, flowers that were thick brush strokes of colour on the canvas of the garden.

Out of the corner of her eye she saw a fluttery grey shape move like a blur into the trees.

"Lyrebird?" she said.

Gone.

But what was that sound? From deep within the forest, she heard a thin, birdlike voice call out, "Goodbye, My Girl Dreaming!"

Neomie awoke later than usual. Lying in her bed, with the sun streaming in stripes through the blinds, she could hear clattering in the kitchen. She lay there a moment, listening. Plates and a cup were clinked carefully in the empty sink, and then a whoosh of water as the dishes were rinsed. Then there was the rattle of the cutlery drawer as things were put away. Must be Mum. It didn't sound like bang-crash Dad at all.

Neomie dressed quickly, brushed her hair and teeth, then ran along the corridor to the kitchen. Dad was at the table, sipping coffee. His plate of bacon and eggs was half finished in front of him, the knife and fork placed together at one side. Dad always ate just enough, never more than he needed. Coffee, on the other hand, was a different matter. He could sit and sip the thick blackness all day.

"Hey, Dad," said Neomie, sitting across from him.

"G'Day, Sport," he said with a wink. Dad could always be relied upon to be Dad.

"Where's Mum?"

"In her studio. As it's Saturday and we ain't working today, I thought we'd let her have some time painting and you and I can go out and so something. We could head into town."

Town was hardly Melbourne, but there'd be some shops. Ice cream, a magazine, maybe. If they picked the right day, the one-screen cinema might have something on that she hadn't seen. There were possibilities.

"Maybe, Dad. Can I talk to Mum first?"

Dad smiled to himself, then picked up his fork. "Seeing as I've got this brekkie to finish, you'd better do that now, before I leave without you."

The air in Mum's studio was fresh. Originally, it was probably built as a conservatory or sunroom, for there were big windows all around its three outside walls, and the open skylight let in the morning sun. It was cool, though, shaded by the garden trees that had grown up along one side. Beyond them was the edge of the forest.

Neomie stood in the doorway, watching her mother painting. She wore a smock over a linen shirt, the sleeves rolled up to the elbows. For the first time, Neomie realised that Mum's view from her studio was the same garden in which she spent most of her time. Although the back door from the kitchen was next to the studio, she hadn't given it much thought, as Mum didn't like her coming in.

Mum was sitting on a stool, with her paints, brushes and water laid out beside her on old table once used for pasting wallpaper. As Neomie watched, she dipped her brush in a blob of blue paint, then dabbed the merest flicker of it onto the canvas in front of her. Neomie's eyes moved from her mother's hands to the painting.

What she saw made her gasp.

The painting, in strong, smiling colours, showed animals and birds dancing around a pool. In the cool pool, fish bobbed, whilst a platypus, a wombat and birds of many shapes and sizes were posed as if dancing around the pool. Amongst the birds were a brolga, a kookaburra, and a lyrebird.

If Mum had heard Neomie, she didn't show it. She carried on painting, adding tiny details to the lyrebird's tail feathers, as Neomie came up behind her. Without saying anything, she placed her hands on her mother's shoulders. Without thinking, she leaned forward and kissed her mother on the top of her head.

Mum turned around. There was a hint of a tear in her eye. She looked up at Neomie from her stool and said, "Hold out your hand".

Neomie held out her hand. Mum placed the handle of the paintbrush in her palm.

"Your turn," she said.

ACKNOWLEDGEMENTS

These stories are drawn together from over several years, but they wouldn't have come about if not for the support of my readers. Thanks therefore go to everyone who supported the Unbound campaign for *A Hundred Years to Arras*, and those who had faith in my earlier small press work.

Printed in Great Britain
by Amazon

77789549R00150